D0090869

BACK TRAIL

**Center Point
Large Print**

Also by Lewis B. Patten
and available from Center Point Large Print:

The Gun of Jesse Hand
The Trial at Apache Junction
Outlaw Canyon

**This Large Print Book carries the
Seal of Approval of N.A.V.H.**

BACK TRAIL

A Western Duo

Lewis B. Patten

CENTER POINT PUBLISHING
THORNDIKE, MAINE

This Center Point Large Print edition
is published in the year 2010 by arrangement with
Golden West Literary Agency.

The text of this Large Print edition is unabridged.
In other aspects, this book may vary
from the original edition.
Printed in the United States of America
on permanent paper.
Set in 16-point Times New Roman type.

ISBN: 978-1-60285-891-6

Library of Congress Cataloging-in-Publication Data

Patten, Lewis B.
  Back trail / Lewis B. Patten.
     p. cm.
  ISBN 978-1-60285-891-6 (lib. bdg. : alk. paper)
  1. Western stories. 2. Large type books.
    I. Patten, Lewis B. His swift and deadly gun hand. II. Title.
  PS3566.A79B33 2010
  813'.54—dc22
                                                    2010020965

Editor's Note

Both of the short novels collected in this book for the first time originally appeared in different magazines. "Back Trail" was published in *Popular Western* (11/53) and "His Swift and Deadly Gun Hand" in *Best Western* (1/54). Although the characters in each story have different names, both stories were purchased by Universal Pictures and served as the basis for *Red Sundown* (Universal-International, 1956) directed by Jack Arnold, starring Rory Calhoun as Alec Longmire, Martha Hyer as Caroline Murphy, Dean Jagger as Jade Murphy, and Robert Middleton as Rufus Henshaw. The screenplay by Martin Berkeley drew on events from both stories, welding them together to form a composite narrative. Despite the differences in character names, "His Swift and Deadly Gun Hand" is really the sequel to "Back Trail". During his lifetime, Lewis B. Patten did not seek to combine these two short novels into a single narrative, as was the case with the film based on them, so they are reprinted now just as he wrote them.

Table of Contents

Back Trail

I

"Flight for Life"

Riding like cavalrymen, they moved across the endless rolling grasslands of Wyoming, crossed the Colorado line climbing, and at dusk of the third day came into the shallow draw that sheltered the vacant and abandoned Mill Iron line camp.

Longmire, tall, slender, and utterly exhausted, swung a stiff, long leg over his saddle and slipped to the ground.

He said, not seeming to care now: "Bud, if they're still on our trail, this is the end of the line. Our horses are beat. They'll drop in another ten miles. I'd say keep the pack horse in the corral and turn the others out to feed."

No man could mistake the plain stamp that was upon these two. Even without the gleaming, well-cared-for twin Colt revolvers that each man carried in snug holsters low along his lusty thighs, the stamp would have been plain enough. In their eyes was the savage gleam of a cornered predator; their movements, even with the stiffness of utter weariness upon them, still retained that odd thriftiness, each movement seeming instantly to accomplish the purpose for which it had been made.

Longmire slipped his saddle from the galled and sweat-plastered back of the bald-faced sorrel, slapped him on the rump, and sent him trotting listlessly down toward the glassy surface of the beaver pond, too tired even to roll. Then he unhooked the panniers from the pack animal, off-saddled him, and turned him into the gray and weathered corral.

Bud Purvis said: "Want to risk a fire? Coffee'd go mighty good tonight."

Longmire shrugged. A man could run only so long. Came a time when he tired of running, put his back on the wall, and fought. Longmire had reached that point.

"Get some wood. I'll clean out the stove and get a fire going."

Purvis, short, stocky, with cold, gray-green eyes, shuffled silently into the timber. Longmire squatted in the doorway, hearing the crack of his knee joints, and took time to roll a wheat-straw cigarette from the soiled and nearly empty sack of Bull Durham he carried in his shirt pocket.

He touched a match to its end, and then, with it dangling from his wide mouth, was utterly and gratefully motionless for a long, long moment.

Longmire carried the gunman's stamp on his mouth—the mouth that had once known how to smile but had lately forgotten—and on his habitually frowning brow. He carried it in his eyes—brown eyes that were startling in their hardness. Yet there were times, rare and unguarded moments, when the hardness left his eyes to be replaced by puzzlement, and hurt, and quiet despair.

You made your big mistake somewhere away back along the line, when you were a kid and took much pride in the way you could shoot. There were always those who tried to top your skill, your school chums, and it became a kind of game, played out to see who was the best at drawing and shooting, at puncturing a tin can tossed high into the air.

You thought that was as far as it was going to go, but when a man packs a gun and knows how to use it, inevitably there comes a time when he does use it. From then on he is a killer.

In Longmire's case, his first killing had not seemed too serious—a tipsy, quarrelsome drifter who had forced a fight upon him too easily, because an eighteen-year-old's pride is strong. Longmire had tried to forget it, and it was patent that his family and the townspeople had also tried to forget it.

Yet one day another stranger hit town, a stranger who bore a faintly unmistakable resemblance to the first one. A brother.

So Alex Longmire had killed his second man in the same dusty street, and holstered his smoking gun, now beginning to see the end of the long, inevitable trail, beginning to feel a little scared.

"Ride out, kid," the sheriff had told him regretfully. "Throw that damned gun away and ride without it."

Perhaps it would have been all right, even then, if he had taken the sheriff's well-meant advice. But he was eighteen and could not see where he had done anything so awfully wrong. Both fights had been forced upon him. He rode out, all right, but with a resentful bravado that made him hang onto his gun.

There had been a third, and a fourth, and a fifth, all clear-cut cases of self-defense. By the time those were behind him he had begun to see the wisdom of the old sheriff's advice. But it had been too late then to throw his gun away. He was known. He had a reputation. He'd been fair game for other gunmen who sought to add fame to their own names. To throw away his gun then would have been suicide.

So he'd bought another gun and labored mightily to improve his skill, the skill that was now his life insurance.

The road had led with frightening inevitability to this cold and abandoned line camp as though each move he made from the very first had been charted and planned, as though he were merely a pawn on fate's chessboard.

He tossed away the cigarette, rose, and went into the moldy-smelling cabin. On the back wall, four bunks were hung from ceiling and log wall. A long table, with one leg broken, occupied the center of the packed and damp dirt floor, and what had once been two benches lay capsized beside it. The stove, a low, sheet-iron affair, was rusty and filled with ashes, but Longmire guessed it would be adequate for a small fire.

With the stove clean, he shoved a stick of dry wood into it, then took a coffee pot from one of the panniers and walked to the beaver pond to fill it. By the time he returned, Purvis was back with a towering armload of wood.

Dark dropped its chill blanket over the land. Unsmiling, unspeaking, the two men drank their steaming coffee and gnawed at their bacon and stale bread between gulps. The fire died, and with it died the little light that had gleamed from the holes in the rusted sides of the stove.

Still the men sat, tired beyond endurance, but putting off sleep. Both knew that sleep, in their present exhausted condition, was a betrayal of watchfulness, tantamount to surrender.

Purvis murmured: "Go ahead. I'll watch till midnight."

"All right."

Longmire stood up, stretched stiffly. He crossed the cabin to the back wall and sat gingerly down on the edge of one of the bunks. He drew his left gun from its holster and, holding it in his right hand, lay down, facing the door. As nights in this high country went, this was a warm one, and he did not now feel the need of the single blanket he carried in a slicker roll behind his saddle.

In the doorway, Purvis's cigarette made a spot of

friendliness, and the odor of the smoke was pleasant and comforting.

Longmire knew he should be sleeping, but tonight, for some reason, he could not help staring down the back trail. From town to town, all over the West he had traveled, unwanted wherever he stopped, growing used to the combination of fear and respect and revulsion that men showed him. He never had much money—only the little he could pick up playing poker—and at the times, when he was broke, he would earn a few dollars with a trail herd, or on a lonely line-riding job.

So far, he had never hired his gun, nor had he stolen, except an occasional horse. Yet, if the trail continued, that was as inevitable as the rest of it. You were a wanted man somewhere; you were broke and hungry. You got to figuring that, if you were wanted for murder, you had just as well be wanted for bank robbery, too. So you threw in with someone else and held up a bank.

The trail had but one ending, an ending you had grown used to. He had read that ending in the old family Bible when he was a boy. "He who lives by the sword shall die by the sword." Only this time it was a gun. A smoothly oiled, carefully cleaned Colt .45.

Some way his thoughts faded before his exhaustion, and he slept, not lightly and nervously tonight, but deeply, restfully. He had made up his mind that this was the end of the trail, and that had its way of relaxing him as nothing else could have done.

Otherwise, he would have wakened sooner. Otherwise, the slight, small noises outside the cabin would have brought him to his feet long before they did. He came awake instantly, completely, yet without a single muscular movement save for the opening of his eyes.

Purvis, his prone form lighted faintly by starlight from the open door, was, Longmire knew, also awake, although the chill in the air, the pre-dawn chill, told Longmire instantly that Purvis had not kept watch as he had agreed to do. Used to telling time by instinct and feel, Longmire placed the time now at about three o'clock.

The night was wholly still, save for the light breeze that played through the boughs of the giant spruces behind the cabin, save for the murmur of water as it ran past the cabin on its way to the still surface of the beaver pond. Longmire could not have said what it was that had wakened him. But he did catch the nervous stirring of the pack horse's hoofs from the corral, the soft flurry of sound as a hand was clamped over the animal's nostrils.

Longmire whispered: "They're here, Bud. For God's sake get out of that doorway."

The prone figure of Purvis stirred, sprang instantly then into violent action. He came to his feet, diving aside at the same time. But he was too late. A rifle made its savage thunder from the shallow ravine through which the stream ran, and Bud Purvis spun around as though struck by a giant fist. The gun he had drawn so smoothly, as he rose, spun from his hand and clattered against the sheet-iron stove.

Longmire sprang around the table to drag Bud's body clear, but Bud remained on his feet, and ducked out of the doorway with a sharply indrawn breath. Longmire stuck his head around the doorjamb and snapped a shot at the place where the rifle had flashed. His bullet must have slapped dirt into the rifleman's open mouth, for, in the midst of the following fusillade, he could hear someone hawking and spitting.

He ignored the bullets, which were wasting themselves in the thick log walls, and spoke to Bud, left hand out to steady him. "Where you hit?"

"Side, gutshot, damn them! Kid, this is the one I've been riding away from all my life."

"Go sit down." Longmire pulled out his shirt tail and tore it off. "Hold this against the wound. Tight."

Purvis staggered to the bunk, face white in the odd, pale glow of starlight. He groaned softly as he sank down.

Longmire asked: "How bad? Can you tell?"

Purvis was silent for a moment, as he tore the clothing away from the wound. His voice, when he spoke, was bitter, and the overtone in it was perhaps a kind of quiet terror.

"Punctured an intestine. I can tell, Alex. Damn them! Damn them! Why can't they kill a man clean?"

Longmire did not answer. Again he put his head around the door casing, but in the almost non-existent light could see nothing at which to shoot.

A voice raised harsh echoes above the whispering wind. "Take it in there by bullets, or come out and get it by a rope at daybreak! It's your choice, boys, but there's no getting away!"

Purvis spoke weakly from the bunk: "Old man Zellman. He must've set a heap of store by that mean kid of his."

Zellman owned fifty sections of Wyoming grass and 10,000 cattle. Rod Zellman, his son, had grown used to throwing the weight that Z Star carried like a whip against lesser men. Longmire hadn't knuckled under, but even so it could have stopped there, for Longmire'd had no inclination to pursue the quarrel further. But the damned fool kid had drawn his iron, backed by a foreman with more loyalty for his brand than good sense.

Longmire could remember turning his back to walk away, figuring this kid for one who liked to run a bluff, who had never killed and who would not kill now. He'd been wrong. Purvis, an older hand at this than he was, had shoved him roughly aside the barest instant before the kid fired.

All hell had broken loose then, Rod Zellman shooting, the foreman shooting, even some of the hands showing an inclination to join the celebration.

Purvis had dropped the foreman with a single shot. Longmire had killed Rod with another, winged the bartender with a second. Then they'd got out of town—fast. Pulling a pack horse behind because they could feel that this trail would be longer than it was fast.

They'd been right, as Longmire was realizing now. The trail had been 700 miles long. And it had ended here in this Mill Iron abandoned line camp.

He said: "Lie down and take it easy. They won't rush us."

No. They wouldn't rush the cabin. They'd be figuring that enough men had been killed and would try to do this without sacrificing any more.

A steady fire began to whine toward the cabin, and a fair scattering of the bullets found their way through the open door. Longmire propped the table against the wall directly beside the door, and helped a weakened but unbeaten Bud Purvis to it.

Why did a man try so hard to stay alive? Why was this instinct for self-preservation so strong? Longmire had nothing to live for, except more of facing men who would try to kill him, except another end exactly like this at some future date. Purvis could have no more.

He kicked a rusted and broken-handled shovel as he moved back across the room to take his stand beside the opposite jamb of the door. His mind kept clawing around in the things he knew, in the things he remembered, trying to find some narrow avenue of escape from this.

Bud Purvis spoke softly from across the room: "Alex, I've got a buckskin bag full of gold double eagles in my pants. I'll never use it. If you get a chance to go, take it. It's six hundred dollars. It might help you out some time."

"All right, Bud." Longmire did not try to kid Purvis, did not try to tell him that it was fiction that he'd be getting out of here. He knew better, and so did Bud.

Purvis groaned, torn by increasing pain: "I ain't got much more time."

"No." Longmire could feel the unfairness of this, the brutal unfairness. "I haven't, either, I guess."

Rod Zellman had purely asked to be killed. So had the others. Longmire had never sought a quarrel, and had often tried his level best to avoid one. Still, you couldn't expect a man just to let someone kill him without even trying to fight back. Longmire never had and never would.

His mind would not relinquish its frantic seeking for escape. He thought: *Hell, there's no way out. They're all around us. If I stepped out that door, a dozen rifles would cut me down.*

He shrugged fatalistically.

Purvis stirred on the table, saying finally— "Catch, Alex."—and tossed the heavy bag of gold across to Longmire. He went on regretfully: "I

21

ain't so sorry about myself. I've rode away from more scrapes than a man's got a right to expect. I hate to see them get you, though, kid. And the damned devils won't even dig you a shallow grave."

Longmire snapped a shot at a dim shadow in the yard, and didn't even care when he missed. There had to be an end to killing somewhere.

Purvis laughed hoarsely. "I must be goin' crazy. I just got the damnedest crazy idea."

"What?" asked Longmire without interest.

"A shallow grave. If we only had a shovel. . . ."

"There's a shovel here. What are you talking about?"

Purvis's voice picked up interest. "It might work. Damn your eyes, it just might work."

"For God's sake, what might work?"

"Get that shovel, kid. Dig yourself a grave about a foot deep. I'll cover you up, and leave one of them rusty tin cans sticking out so's you can breathe."

"There'd be dirt left over. That wouldn't fool anybody."

"Put the dirt in the stove, and cover it up with ashes."

"They'd notice the fresh dirt. Forget it, Bud."

Longmire felt a little sorry for Bud. Pain was beginning to affect his mind.

But Bud was becoming insistent. "I got away from a posse once on Grand River, laying in the

22

water and breathing by holding my nose out of water under a grass overhang on the bank. It's what gave me this idea. You got nothing to lose, kid. Give it a try."

Longmire, still protesting, but no longer with the same conviction, said: "I could only cover myself to the waist. You ain't strong enough to finish it."

"The hell I ain't. Get busy, Alex. It's like trying to draw to an inside straight. You ain't got much chance, but it's been done."

Longmire shrugged, finally groped and found the shovel. The chance was slim, all right. But Purvis was right. It was a chance.

Longmire said: "All right. I'll try it. You can turn the table over on top of me, and maybe hide the fresh dirt. But if they find me, it won't be a bullet I'll get. It'll be a rope."

II

"Tried by Fire"

Before dawn raised smoky gray from the eastern horizon, Zellman sent his riders in behind the cabin with dry wood and firebrands. But Purvis kept the wedge-shaped area before the door clear with the deadly fire of his .45s.

Longmire, even though lacking confidence in Bud's plan, dug with the rusty shovel at the hard-dirt floor. Carefully he carried what he judged would be surplus dirt to the stove, carefully dumped it inside.

Fire caught in the dry brush that underlaid the sod on the roof, and it flamed hotly. Falling brands set Longmire's clothes afire, singed his hair clear to the scalp, cleaned off his eyebrows and mustache as neatly as any razor would have done. He soaked a rag in what coffee remained in the pot and wound this around Purvis's head and face. Then he crawled into his grave and carefully covered himself as far as the waist.

Lying back, doubtfully eyeing the weakened Purvis, he said: "You strong enough?"

"Sure."

"I feel like I'm running out on you."

Purvis grunted: "Why the hell should you feel like that? You ever hear of anybody that made it with a bullet in his guts? Lie down and shut up."

Longmire did. Purvis crawled over to him and began shoving dirt into the grave, covering Longmire's chest and neck. Purvis was growing weaker, growing weaker all the time. He patted and packed the dirt down as he went, until finally all that remained was Longmire's head. Occasionally Purvis would raise up from behind the table that sheltered them from the view of those outside, and fire a couple of carefully placed shots through the doorway.

The fire grew hotter as the log walls caught. The pole beams that supported the ceiling caught fire, weakened and sagged with the weight of sod upon them. Purvis adjusted a tin can with a rusted bottom over Longmire's nose and mouth, then shoveled dirt in around it.

Longmire closed his eyes and strove to fight the panic that crowded over him. Buried alive! Buried alive! His face, the vicious, cruel burns on his face cooled and eased as the damp, wet earth touched him. He could feel the steady patting motion as Purvis smoothed the dirt over him. He heard Purvis's muffled voice, speaking close to the can: "They'll never find you. It was a good idea. The roof's coming down in a minute. Good luck, kid."

Longmire sensed, rather than felt, the motion Purvis made rising. He felt the weight of the table ease down atop his shallow grave. A few seconds later he heard the sharp, short, and vicious volley of shots outside the cabin, and thought Purvis had gone outside. Well, maybe that's easier than burning to death.

The shooting did not stop, and Longmire knew what it was now. Purvis was down. Purvis was dead. Yet still they pumped lead into his inert carcass, raging, vengeful.

A great fury boiled in Longmire. *He's dead! He's dead! Damn you, let him alone!*

But the shooting was slow in stopping, and Longmire could not help flinching at each report. At last even Zellman must have been sated, for the firing stopped.

Now the hard part began, the waiting, the motionless, endless waiting. Earth pressed upon him from all sides. His legs cramped. He could not get enough air, and what he did get was hot and filled with smoke. *Can't cough!* he thought frantically. *Can't cough!*

Dimly he heard the crash of the sod roof, vaguely he felt it in increased weight upon him. He began to sweat from the warmth in the ground about him. The heat scared him, but so did that weight. He thought with a touch of panic—*What if I can't get up?*—and almost tried to then and there.

Yet for years he had disciplined himself. Now that self-discipline repaid him well. He lay utterly quiet for what seemed an eternity, and at last heard the voices of Zellman's posse talking, their tramping about through the smoking rubble of what had been the Mill Iron line camp.

He began to count, more accurately to gauge the passage of time. The voices faded and went away, yet still Longmire lay motionless. They knew they had been following two men as far as this cabin. They would be unable to see how he could have escaped from it. They would begin to wonder if he had not peeled off from Purvis somewhere far back along that 700-mile trail, while Purvis continued on with all of the horses.

They would curse and rave and shout with frustration, for Longmire was the one they wanted. Longmire had fired the shot into Rod Zellman. But eventually they would go away.

Longmire thought: *Give them until mid-afternoon.* And forced a continued relaxation from his tense, his intolerably tense body.

Just before noon they came back, for he could hear their voices and could also hear them digging in the rubble of the sod roof.

They figure I'm buried under the roof, he decided.

Now the tension came back. He felt the thump of a shovel on the table that covered him. He felt the table move then and, sweating profusely, felt it settle back.

Half an hour passed, and again the voices and movements were gone. Pain returned to the burns on Longmire's face and head, burning, searing, blinding pain. The pain made him nervous and jumpy.

He thought: *I'm going to get up. I'm going to try. Anything is better than this.*

Yet the thought of Purvis, of Purvis's cheerful sacrifice held him still for another half hour.

At last, judging it was safe as it would ever be, Longmire gathered his cramped and aching muscles and forced upward with his arms that had been buried folded across his chest so that, when the time came to break free, he would have the purchase and strength to do it.

For an instant there was no give in the weight above him. Panic sent its coursing messages through his body, adding strength to cramped muscles, and at last he felt his arms break through. With his hands, he clawed at the dirt that covered his face, shoved it aside from his body. He raised his head, and shook the dirt from it, wiped dirt from his eyes, and finally opened them.

The table top lay propped six inches from his face. His face was blistered and raw. He freed his legs, and finally rolled on his side. Now he took time, carefully listening, to ease first one gun from a holster, then the other. These he cleaned and checked them carefully, blowing the dirt out of the barrels.

Ready at last, with a gun in each hand, he put his shoulder against the table top and raised against it.

It was heavy. Atop it lay eight inches of sod from

the roof, blackened and dry, but almost too heavy to lift. Longmire raised the table as far as he could, then shifted his body to one side.

He raised and shifted, raised and shifted, until at last he rolled clear, against the still smoldering wall of the cabin.

Now he dared a look over the table and its accumulated load of sod. Sun beat down inside the blackened walls, making a pool of blazing heat within the cabin. Longmire's burns, so long kept cool by the earth around him, set up their awful, racking clamor for attention.

He saw nothing outside the cabin, he heard no stamp of corralled horses, no voices.

He stood up, and moved carefully through the ashes and ruins to the gaping doorway. They were gone. They were gone.

Purvis's body lay face up, staring sightlessly at the blue of the sky. Anger darkened Longmire's thoughts, and the need for revenge was born, but he forced this away from him. There would be no revenge for this, wrong though it may have been. Trouble had its way of finding men like Longmire. They had no need to seek it. If it had not been Zellman, it would have been someone else. Purvis had been marked, as Longmire was marked. This was but a brief respite.

Although every movement was torture, Longmire tramped back to the cabin, dug out the rusted old shovel, and made for Purvis a shallow grave. Afterward, he slogged down to the beaver pond and waded out into it fully dressed. He bathed the dirt carefully from the raw and open blisters on his head and neck and face.

Then, whimpering softly from pain, but with no other outward sign of it, he shuffled away from the cabin and into the timber.

III

"New Identity"

Perhaps Longmire should not have survived. But he did survive. The summer passed and the first frost of October turned the quakie leaves on the high slopes to pure, shining gold.

Deer shed their hard fat from the summer's plenty. The big bucks turned a steely, smoky gray, and rubbed the last of their horn velvet off on the gnarled, low-hanging branches of the cedars.

Wind, cold wind, sighed through the pine boughs, and slate-gray clouds scudded across the sky. Ducks and Canada honkers drove their undulating wedges through the high air toward the south.

Winter, with its days of driving snow, of sub-zero wind, of occasional mild sunshine, also passed. Spring came, a time of balmy days, of new, green grass—a time for spotted fawns and woolly bear cubs and coyote pups. And the ducks and geese came back, flying north.

Longmire had realized during the long months he had spent hiding in a rim-rock cave that this was, perhaps, the only chance he would ever have of exchanging his identity as Alex Longmire, of exchanging with it the painful past and its inexorable demands on the future, for forgetfulness, for a new beginning.

His hair, burned off by the fire, grew in darker and thinner, for apparently the fire had damaged something in its root ends. His face, although not particularly disfigured, was no longer the face of Alex Longmire. The skin, healing, had given the face new contours by virtue of its strange new tightness.

Before the onslaught of winter he had put away his guns. He had used the $600 in gold that Purvis had given him to buy a ranch, this tiny valley ranch with its ten head of white-faced cattle that was now his home.

He had become acquainted with the valley folk, and made them his friends. He had courted Edie Sheridan.

Now, tall, young, with deeply tanned skin that stretched, oddly tight, across his bony, high-cheeked face, he paused in the act of driving a staple in a new cedar fence post to keen the wind that moved over him like a light, warm caress from downcountry.

The sounds he heard were unmistakable enough, yet his mind would not accept them. The sounds were those of sheep bleating, dogs barking, men shouting. The sounds were trouble, and a frown darkened Longmire's brow.

The frown deepened as a new sound struck his listening ears. This was the sound made by horsemen, by galloping hoofs. A bunch of Mill Iron riders swept around a bend in the road, thundering recklessly toward him. Longmire straightened, the wire gate he had been building lying unfinished at his feet.

His new name, Art Lyman, still fell, when used, on ears unaccustomed to its unfamiliar sound—his own ears. Bull-broad Josh Hiatt, owner of the Mill Iron, used it now, harshly.

"Don't let them through, Lyman! Don't let them through. There's fifty thousand acres of grass above you that belongs to the Mill Iron. Damn them, they want to sheep it all off!"

"Who does?"

"Le Clair. Can't you hear them? Stinking woolly critters!"

"Ain't part of that grass Le Clair's?"

"Sure . . . for cattle. Not for sheep."

Hiatt sat his saddle, broad of body, broad of face, a heavy-jawed, implacable man, a man used to giving orders and having them obeyed.

Environment and training had given Longmire an ingrained dislike for sheep and the men who ran them. Environment and training had also given him his core of stubbornness. He felt a stir of anger. His voice, when he spoke, was flat and blunt.

"Hiatt, don't use me to do your dirty work. If you want them stopped, stop them yourself before they get to this gate."

Hiatt's face reddened and for the barest instant he was silent. Before he could speak, another voice, a familiar and well-liked one, pushed into the argument with quiet insistence. "Art's right, Josh. We've got no right to bring him into our quarrel with Le Clair."

Longmire looked at Frank Sheridan, tall, slender, aging, and said: "Hello, Frank. I'll stop them, if it's what you want."

Sheridan, although dressed as were the others, nevertheless did not belong, for his was the quiet, studious face of a thinker. Longmire did not find it hard to imagine Frank Sheridan in a still, soft-lit study, surrounded by books. Instead, his present dress and his presence upon a plunging black in the midst of these other riders were incongruities.

Josh Hiatt growled intemperately: "All right . . . stop them!"

Longmire grinned without mirth. "Not for you, Hiatt. Not for you."

Sheridan's face was tight with worry. He asked: "Stay out of it, Art."

Josh Hiatt growled: "Damn it, Frank, it will make it easier for all of us if Lyman stops them. His fence runs from rim to rim. Le Clair's beat if Lyman turns him back."

"Le Clair's determined, Josh. You want to shove your quarrel off onto Art's hands?"

"It's his quarrel, too. Le Clair will grub him out, crossing his land. This is cattle country. It's every cattleman's quarrel when sheep move in."

Hiatt rode close to Longmire, looking down, using his bulk and the height of his horse to enforce his demand. "Lyman, I'm telling you for the last time, turn them back! Mill Iron only tolerates you damned two-bit ranchers anyway. Mill Iron can break you any time."

Longmire grinned insolently. "Go to hell."

The vanguard of the band of sheep came around the bend and, seeing horsemen, stopped. The sheep behind the leaders bunched, bleating. A man rode around the bunch, approaching swiftly. With this man—Hector Le Clair—in hearing, Hiatt gave his crew swift and succinct orders.

"Ride through Lyman's place! Take a stand outside his fence on the other side. If sheep come through, kill them! Kill every critter that steps off Lyman's land." He turned toward Longmire, grinning triumphantly, his stance and his expression saying plainly: *I don't need you, but you'd have been smart to play along.*

Longmire shrugged.

Sheridan spoke up with instant concern. "Josh, are you ready for this? Are you ready to go this far?"

"You're damned right I am! Frank, you're a fool. This flock of sheep is Le Clair's opening wedge. If I let them through, how long do you think he'll wait before he brings in more?"

Le Clair, dark, short, Gallic-quick, rode nervously close, his black eyes angry but well-controlled.

"Josh"—his voice was strongly accented—"we are friends, you and me."

"No more! I warned you not to bring your sheep in here. Now turn them back before they all get killed."

"I do not want your grass. I only want what is mine."

Hiatt snorted intolerantly. "Never was a damned sheepman that could take what was his and no more. My cattle won't graze where sheep have been. The stink is worse in their noses than it is in mine. You turn back, Le Clair. You turn back, or there'll be dead sheep in the valley . . . and dead men, too!"

Sheridan spoke regretfully. "He means it, Le Clair."

Le Clair's sharp, Gallic face tightened with help-less anger. "I have grass in this valley. I have sheep to eat it. I promise you that they will eat it. Sheridan, you know I am right. You should stand on the side that is right."

Frank Sheridan's expression seemed to settle. He murmured: "Perhaps you are. Perhaps not. The fact remains that you are the one who is stir-ring up the trouble. You have always run cattle before. Why the sudden change? You know that cattle won't graze where sheep have been. You have always run cattle in the valley, and part of the grass is yours. But not for sheep, Le Clair. Not for sheep."

Le Clair shrugged eloquently. His voice assumed an ironic tone, which was not at all defeated. "Tonight, you win. Tomorrow. . . ." He shrugged again, whirled his horse, and rode away.

Hiatt rumbled: "Why that Basque son-of-a-bitch. Threaten me, will he?" He started to follow, but Frank Sheridan stopped him with a curt: "Josh."

Hiatt raged: "To hell with you! We'll settle this once and for all right now!"

Longmire, familiar with this, could see the hair-trigger closeness of gun play and death.

Sheridan flung his voice into the breach frantically. "Josh, dead men in the valley can't settle anything. Live men can, if they try! Leave your men where they are tonight, if it will make you feel any better. But come away yourself and give the thing time to cool off."

"And give him time to bring his gunslinger in from Utah?"

"Josh, that's only a rumor. You don't know that Le Clair has hired Chet Swann."

Chet Swann. The name was known to Longmire, too. Swann did what Longmire had never done—hired his gun, killed for pay. Swann would open the valley for Le Clair all right, but would open it over the bodies of half a dozen good men.

Damn this hot-headed, bull-headed breed of man anyway, this breed that had peopled the West! Both Le Clair and Hiatt figured they were right. They'd go all the way down any road to prove it. They'd back their opinions with their guns, and, when it was over. . . .

Longmire shrugged. To hell with it. It was not his quarrel. He would not make it his quarrel. Let them fight. Let them kill each other. Let the winner take the grass. There could be no other way, for this was the way these things were settled.

Hiatt, already uncertain, yielded at last, saying in his grumbling, unconvinced way: "Well, tonight then, Frank. But no more than that."

He rode through Longmire's gate, rode in the direction his own men had taken, and disappeared into the scattering timber.

Frank Sheridan, left alone with Longmire, said: "When Edie learned I was to be up here today, she told me to bring you to supper. She says you're too skinny, but only from eating your own cooking."

"Can you wait while I shave and saddle a horse?"

"Sure. I'll be here at the gate. I want to ride after Josh and talk to him for a minute, anyway."

Longmire gave him a grin, picked up his tools, and strode through the timber toward his cabin.

IV

"A Woman for a Man"

Longmire was jumpy, and he was nervous. That was what gun talk could do to him. His muscles felt like wires, tightly strung on his bony frame. In his head was the soaring recklessness that this tension always engendered. He was a cocked and loaded .45, his life balancing on the hair-trigger.

This was another thing that the fighting years did to a man. Fighting became an intoxicant in his bloodstream. Longmire thought he had put it all away. He found suddenly that it was to be harder than that.

Yet all he needed to calm himself was a long look down the back trail. A look at the bodies lying strewn along it was all he had ever needed. And if that failed him, he could look ahead, could walk among those who were yet to die by his gun until he came to his own body, lying in death's awkwardness, perforated with lead and bleeding into the thirsty dust.

He made himself relax; he made himself think of Edie Sheridan. He had met Frank Sheridan that first fall, as Frank had been riding out of the upper valley driving his gather before him. Frank was one of the smaller ranchers, running less than 200 head on the grass of the upper valley.

As a neighborly gesture Frank had invited Longmire to supper, and Longmire had saddled up and helped him drive his gather of forty or fifty cattle down the road. He remembered Edie, standing on the verandah, leaning a little into the brisk fall wind, her long skirts billowing about her slender body.

Edie Sheridan was all of the things a man missed riding alone. She was gentleness, serenity, and sanctuary from the storm. She was the fire that warmed the hearth of a man's heart. She was the reason for being. She could be lightning, flashing out of a somber sky. She could be the slow, silent depth of the river, mysterious and unrevealing. She could be the reason that the wildness in Longmire had died so willingly.

Now he scrambled out of his clothes, picked up a bar of soap and a towel, and walked, naked, to the creek. Skinny, Edie had said, but she had never seen him like this. His shoulders were broad, his belly flat and corded with muscle, his hips slender. Not an ounce of flesh to spare, all of it being muscle—long, flat muscle with the strength and resiliency of rawhide.

His skin was white, milk white below the bronze circle of neckline. A bullet scar was across his ribs, angry and red after two years, and across the smooth muscles of his shoulder another had left a lump of proud flesh.

He scrubbed himself briskly in the cold water of

the creek, went back to the cabin, and scraped the two-day growth of whiskers from his face. He dressed in clean clothes, saddled his horse, mounted, and rode to the gate where Frank Sheridan was waiting for him.

The sheep had been withdrawn from his gate. They had spread out and were grazing the rising slopes on the eastern side of the valley. Le Clair's herders had erected a tent and from it issued the smell of wood smoke, coffee, and frying meat.

Sheridan said: "Le Clair rode downcountry. I'm afraid what Josh said about Chet Swann may be true."

Longmire shrugged. "So it's true. I've seen sheep come into a country before, Frank. It ain't the end of the world. There's a flurry of fighting, but the sheepmen always win."

"Why?"

"I'll be damned if I know. Maybe because they keep on trying. Maybe because they feel they've got a right to live, same as everyone else does."

"Le Clair shouldn't have hired a gunman."

A wry grin creased Longmire's wide mouth. "Is there another way to handle Josh Hiatt's kind?"

"No. I guess not. There is only one trouble. I'll have to back Hiatt. I run my cattle in the upper valley with his. His fight will have to be my fight, too."

The age difference between these two seemed suddenly to evaporate. The respect Longmire felt for Edie's father was gone as well before the urgency of the moment. He said intemperately: "Frank, don't be such a damned fool! I know Swann. I've seen his gun work. Neither a man like Hiatt nor like you has any chance at all against him. You might just as well blow out your own brains as go up against him."

Sheridan shrugged. "Swann isn't here yet, and there's no use worrying about him until he is. Forget it."

Longmire couldn't forget it. Long experience had shown him the pattern of these things. Hiatt and Sheridan would take their stand on the north fence of Longmire's place. Le Clair would drive on through, but Swann would be in the vanguard, Swann, the gunman whose start had perhaps been accidental like Longmire's, but who had traveled the road farther. Swann had reached the point, long ago, when he had realized that, branded with the killer stamp forever, he had just as well make it give him a few of life's comforts.

Swann was cold, passionless. Killing had become his business. Longmire felt a growing anger.

"Frank," he said, "Hiatt runs over two thousand cattle in the valley. Le Clair has run as many as a thousand. It's their fight. You stay to hell out of it and let them settle it between themselves."

Sheridan grunted and conceded: "You make sense. I'm the one that doesn't."

Longmire felt relieved.

Steadily their horses put the miles behind. The unbroken rims flowed past. The sprawl of Hiatt's ranch buildings grew to reality from a series of distance-shrouded specks before them. A utility ranch, its untidiness the untidiness of a working place.

Hiatt's wife, a small, pert wren of a woman, gave them a neighborly wave from the front stoop of the ranch house. Hiatt's two boys—young Josh, who was eight, and Tammy, four—stopped their play to stare.

Hiatt's hay fields, bright with new, short alfalfa growth, stretched away from the house and out-buildings, green, lush, and promising. Irrigation water, sheening over parts of the fields, reflected the bronze glow of the dying sun.

Farther downcreek, bordering Hiatt's lower field, stretched the ranch of Le Clair, which was different, yet strangely the same.

Longmire asked: "Why the sudden switch to sheep? He was doing all right with cattle."

"He's a Frenchman, a Basque. Sheep are his heritage. For a hundred generations his ancestors have tended flocks. Cattle have made him a fair living, but the sheep are in his blood, and the sheep will make him rich."

Behind them, Hiatt and a couple of his riders turned in at Hiatt's gate, riding stiff, riding straight, with an unconscious pride in themselves when a fight is in prospect. Prospect of fighting could always inflame men, but that was before they had seen as much of fighting's aftermath as Longmire had.

Men who had faced as much of fighting as had Longmire quickly sickened of it, for no fight has a winner. In those who live must always be remorse, the nausea of futility, and often the surrender of the very principles for which they fought. The dead left bitterness behind, bitterness in those who had loved and depended upon them. The cripples nurtured memory in their twisted bodies.

Thinking aloud, Longmire said: "The valley could be divided easily enough. Why does a man have to be born so damned stubborn?"

Sheridan shrugged, smiling ruefully. "It's not stubbornness always. It's a man's knowledge that, if he ever surrenders to force, he will never be able to stop surrendering. Tolerance, in this world, is interpreted as weakness. Therefore, a man must never allow himself to show it." There was bitterness in Sheridan's words that betrayed his own personal experience.

Two miles below Le Clair's broad fields were Sheridan's smaller ones. The sun was down, and early dusk, softly violet, laid its serenity over the land. A pleasant time of day, thought Longmire, a time when a man could lay aside his labors and turn toward the richness of the thing he worked for—four walls that sheltered his dreams, that prisoned gently the woman who gave his life meaning.

Edie Sheridan was waiting for him to speak, he knew, and only the past reared a wall between them.

They rode into the yard, and Longmire lifted an arm toward Edie in the kitchen doorway. At the corral they dismounted, the graying old man, the dark-haired young one. Sheridan forked hay down to the horses, grinning.

"Man," he said, "I wish you'd come oftener for dinner. Edie really spreads herself for you." But constraint touched him almost immediately, as he obviously realized he was pushing something he had no right to push.

Longmire ducked his head under the pump, ran a comb through his hair, and strode with rising anticipation toward the door. Tactfully Sheridan did not follow, having just recalled some chore yet undone.

There was shyness in Edie, but her softly full lips curved with pleasure. "Hello, Art. I'm glad you could come. Supper will be ready in a minute."

He lounged in the doorway, big, slim, full of indolence and relaxation that concealed his intensity, his overpowering desire to take her in his arms. He let his eyes run over her in a way that was personal and demanding, yet tender, too. He saw the high-piled, dark, and gleaming hair that accentuated the whiteness of her face, of her proud neck column. He saw the beat of quickened pulse in the hollow of her throat, the rise and fall of her breasts. He saw the slim strength of her body. . . .

And he saw the startled fright in her eyes, fright that beckoned and pushed away, a seeming inconsistency. Her smile weakened and died.

A long stride put him close to her and his arms went out. Slight she was, rounded and soft. In his arms she was alive, strong. Her face lifted for his kiss.

Longmire's past had kept him aloof from her. Until tonight. Women do not understand the men in whose grasp lies so much sudden death. Always before he had feared, above all else, to see upon Edie's lovely face the horror, the terror, the undiluted disgust he had so often seen upon other women's faces.

Tonight that fear was gone. Her body in his arms brought to him, more than ever before, the full realization that man and woman cannot drift. Man and woman relationship is not a drifting one.

Tonight, Edie must know what he was, what he had been. She must weigh Art Lyman against Alex Longmire. She must weigh this new man against the old.

Her lips were soft, at the same time firm and demanding. Her body arched against him, and his blood ran hot and fast.

Hoarsely he whispered: "I've got to have you, Edie! I've got to have you!"

A murmur, words formed out of soft, fragrant breath: "Oh, yes, darling! Yes. Yes."

This would be so easy. Alex Longmire was dead. He had perished in the Mill Iron's gutted and abandoned line camp. Why must he tell Edie of Alex Longmire at all? Why could not Longmire and the things Longmire had been die decently?

Edie asked: "Can I tell Dad?"

Almost Longmire nodded. Almost. Then he saw the wall rearing between them, a wall that might at times be penetrated by man and wife, but a wall that would endure. He shook his head.

"There are things you do not know about me. There are things you have to know. There are the things I have done before I came to your valley."

Hers was a gentle pity, a woman's pity. Her soft palm stroked the unruliness of his hair, the scars on his face. She said: "I know what you are now. What you have been no longer matters."

He shrugged, and stepped away. If he had decided upon reticence, she would have respected his reticence. But the nature of woman is essentially curious. Loving him, she would want to know everything about him.

He heard Frank Sheridan's step on the stoop, the squeak of the door as it opened. Edie brushed a wisp of hair from her forehead and busied herself with the rolls, browning in the oven, with the chicken, crisping atop the stove.

47

Light sweat beaded on Longmire's brow. There was warmth in Edie's soft eyes for him now, a woman's love. What would be there when he had shown her the men who had fallen before his smoking gun? What would be there, then?

V
"I Am a Killer"

In the hot and steamy kitchen, Longmire sat at the dinner table, forking the delicious food into his mouth that Edie had prepared like it was so much oatmeal mush. The sweat seemed to pour more heavily from his pores, and once he dragged the clean bandanna from his pocket and mopped it away from his forehead.

"Dad, it's too hot in here. Open the door." Edie's voice showed concern, and Longmire gave her a smile that was meant to be polite and reassuring, but only succeeded in being scared.

He didn't like this. He didn't like it at all. All of a sudden it had struck him forcefully how brutal must be his words to her, however he phrased them—*Edie, I'm a killer. I've killed seven men.* Almost like bragging. Almost like he was proud of it.

He had to do it differently than that. He had to make her see. He had to make her see the eighteen-year-old, proud of the gun his father had given him, proud of his skill with it, proud because he could put two holes in a can while it tumbled earthward, and the best any of the others could do was one.

He had to make her see the first one, the tipsy

drifter, the man who had been so sarcastically scornful of the gun Longmire carried. He had to make Edie see how that scorn, combined with a boy's volatile pride, had built itself into a quarrel. If the man had only been sober, he would have seen the danger signs in the boy. But he hadn't been sober.

Edie said reproachfully: "Art, don't you like my cooking? You're hardly eating a thing."

"Hmm? Sorry. Sure, I like it." And he grabbed a golden piece of breast from the plate she held before him.

His face flushed painfully as he felt her eyes upon him, but he could not stop his thoughts. The second, the drifter's brother seeking revenge.

Perhaps that one would be explained easier. Longmire didn't know. That one had come, plainly seeking him, plainly avowing a desire for revenge. Longmire had been at the stable, squatted on his heels in the shade, talking to old Si Deane. One of the kids he ran with, Sammy Ritter, had come running up from the saloon with the breathless news: "Alex, his brother's here . . . he's looking for you! Alex, you better run or he'll kill you!"

Pride again. Edie would ask: "Why didn't you run, Art?"

Why hadn't he? That heady feeling that all eyes were upon him. The intoxication of being looked upon as a man, a grown man and a dangerous one. Vanity. Pride. And perhaps, deep down underneath, a better reason—the knowledge that running would not make the man peel off from his trail. Yet he would have to make Edie see it all, see all of the reasons, not just the favorable ones.

He'd have to make her see why he hadn't thrown away his guns after that one. Pride again—not the admirable kind of pride that backs a principle, but stubborn pride, bull-headed, kid pride.

The third one had been a gambler, a smooth, suave one who had thought he could cheat a kid and back the cheat with a bluff. The gambler's vest pocket Derringer had been little protection against Longmire's .45, yet it was the gambler's Derringer that had given him the raw, red scar across his ribs.

The fourth, another kid, hardly older than himself, laughing, reckless, deliberately provoking a shoot-out to see if Longmire was as good as he was supposed to be. The fifth—oh, hell, what was the use of going along the line any further?

Looking back, it was increasingly hard for Longmire to find real justification in any of them. One fact only remained in his confused mind. If it had not been them, it would have been him. If any one of the seven still lived, then Longmire himself would be dead.

Edie was clearing away the dishes, and both she and her father were watching Longmire strangely. Longmire gave her a twisted smile as she set a wedge of steaming apple pie before him, and his smile erased some of the worried concern from her eyes.

He could tell her now, and perhaps he would be fairer to her if he did. In the brightly lighted kitchen Longmire's words would fall, stark and cruel, from his lips, to be judged not by Edie alone, but by Edie and her father together, thinking as one, making their decision as one.

Yet he made this one concession to himself. He would wait. He would tell her later when he had her to himself outside in the soft and fragrant spring night. Her decision must be hers alone, and not colored by what she thought her father's decision would be.

Longmire thought bitterly: *I've erased the past. This year I have spent here has erased the past.*

But he could recall the wildness that had flared in him this afternoon, wildness born of gun talk and impending violence. He knew that the battle was only half won. He would always need a cruel curb bit in his mouth and a strong hand at the reins.

The pie was finished, and the strong black coffee with it. Frank Sheridan excused himself and retired to his little study with a cigar. Longmire idly puffed his own cigar and watched Edie's quick, slight hands at their task of washing dishes. His eyes upon her raised pink to her face. At last, laughing, he rose and took the dishtowel from her hands.

Closeness, and this small, domestic task, brought

a delicious sense of intimacy to them both. Crossing behind her, Longmire leaned down and kissed the warm nape of her neck.

The violence of her response startled him. She whirled, forgetting the white suds that covered her arms to the elbows. Her hands flew about his neck and her body was flung against him. Her lips, full and warm and slightly parted, sought his own.

Spontaneous, sweet, heartbreakingly natural and tender. A woman gesture compounded of love, and desire, and the knowledge that waiting was past. Sweet and all too brief. Realizing that she had drenched his neck and back with suds, she broke away, dismayed. Then she began to laugh. Longmire could only laugh with her, and their merriment rolled through the house, penetrated Sheridan's study, and brought a contented smile to the old man's lips.

Edie took Longmire firmly by his arm, led him back to his chair. "You stay here," she scolded. "Dishwashing is woman's work. Besides, I can do it faster without you than with you."

Longmire watched her and wished this work were done, wished he could take her arm and lead her outside into the night. He could see the same desire in her own eyes, along with a touch of fright at the prospect. Her hands fairly flew as they went about their work.

At last she dried her hands and took off her apron. "There. Shall we go in?"

He grinned. "Out. Come on."

Only a few steps from the door. Only a few steps, and then excitement brought them both around, into a quick embrace. Woman's eternal invitation of protest. Longmire's sudden withdrawal, his words.

"Edie, I love you. I want to marry you. But I've got to tell you about myself before you give me your answer."

"I have given you my answer, Art."

"No. Listen. I'm not Art Lyman. My name is Alex Longmire."

"Art. Alex. Darling, be still. What does it matter? I did not fall in love with the man you used to be. I fell in love with you . . . with you, as you are now." Her palm sought to cover his mouth.

He put it gently away. "No. I'm a killer, Edie. I'm a gunman. It is not only one man behind me. It is. . . ." How could a single word be so hard to tear from your throat? "Seven, Edie. Seven."

She was so still, so silent, so unmoving. Why had he told her at all? Were not some things best kept forever secret, even from those you loved the best? His body unconsciously stiffened. The warmth of the night turned chill; the sounds and the smells drifting in so lightly on the breeze became unpleasant, even threatening.

He shrugged, a bitter gesture of defiance. He started to turn away, but the shaking, the cruel shaking of her body stopped him. She was crying, silently, bitterly, almost tearlessly.

"Edie, don't! Please! I'll go away. You'll never see me again." The defiance was gone, the bitterness with it.

Her voice was hardly audible. "I have never seen you carry a gun. I have never seen you angry. I've seen what you really are in the year you've been here. What you were before was only what other men made of you." Her face was flushed, white, defiant, but holding no blame, only shock, and hurt, and perhaps pity. "Is the law after you?"

"No. Not the law."

He told her then. He told her of the burned-out Mill Iron line camp, of Purvis, of the months spent like a wolf in a rim-rock cave. He told her that he was safe from the violence within him.

As he talked, they walked. Up the lane to the road, down the road a full two miles and back. The moon rose and moved across the sky.

At midnight he left her at her home and rode out. He left her a woman grown, still loving, still wanting, but torn by the pain of life's harshness. He had led her away from her door a girl; he had returned her to it a woman, fully matured in these few short hours.

And he left with the self-given promise that pain should never touch her again.

VI

"Little Lost Boy"

Up at daybreak, Longmire hurried through his chores so that he could ride, early, down the road toward Sheridan's. His spirits were high, higher than he could ever remember them. He sang, and he whistled. He laughed aloud as his dun saddle horse bucked and tossed the morning chill out of his powerful body.

Even the sheep, gray spots that speckled the hillside, could not dampen his cheerfulness today. A Basque sheepherder, mustached and graying, looked up warily at Longmire's approach, rifle cradled in his arms. Longmire lifted a hand, and this, coupled with the fact that Longmire's lean thighs bore no holstered guns, drew a wide grin from the man, and an answering wave.

Yet in spite of his hurrying, it was past eight when Longmire rode abreast of Josh Hiatt's big spread. Unwonted activity in fields and yard brought a puzzled frown to his face. Riders moved aimlessly and hurriedly back and forth across the fields.

In the yard he could see Mrs. Hiatt, wren-tiny, scurrying back and forth, accomplishing nothing, apparently trying to accomplish nothing. Her shrill voice lifted on the warm spring air, its

56

frantic tone clearly distinguishable, if the words were not.

Longmire's frown deepened, and he stopped, watching the mounting confusion. Then, plainly, clearly, he heard Josh Hiatt's bull voice: "Tammy! Tammy! Damn it, boy, where are you?"

Longmire had been thinking about Le Clair, of the threat he presented to the peace of the valley. Unconsciously his mind had coupled Le Clair with the confusion in Hiatt's yard.

Now he grinned with quick relief, as he thought: *Boy's lost, and they're excited.*

Tammy Hiatt, at four, had reached the age when an exploring urge could hit him at any time. Tammy's real name was Sammy, but since young Josh had not been able to form an "S" at the time of Sammy's birth, he had called him Tammy, and the name had stuck.

Longmire could not feel the same concern over the boy that the parents apparently were feeling. The weather was warm. It was too early for snakes. There was nothing to hurt Tammy. Yet friendly instinct turned him in at Hiatt's gate to offer his help.

He angled at once across the field to intercept one of Hiatt's riders, a round and jolly man known as Tubby.

"Boy lost, Tubby?"

"Uhn-huh." Tubby was riding across an open field, a field in which you could have seen a rabbit, peering to right and left assiduously. His face was round and full of worried concern.

"How long's he been gone?"

"Hell, that's the funny part. We don't know. The little booger must've slipped out of his bed early. His clothes is gone, so he must've dressed hisself. Josh weren't worried much till breakfast time, 'cause Tammy's done this before. Then he commenced to wonder where the kid was. He done a little hunting, and then he begun to get scared."

"Don't you reckon you'd find him quicker if you'd sort of organize the search?"

Tubby snorted. "Sure. But you try telling Hiatt that. I won't. He's fit to be tied."

Longmire grinned. "Like your job, huh? All right, I'll tell him. I've got nothing to lose."

He rode toward the house at a slow canter, but as he approached it, his grin faded. There was something so terribly anguished about Hiatt's wife, something so terribly helpless. Josh Hiatt stood beside her, alternately bellowing ill-considered orders and taking her into his thick arms to pat her shoulder clumsily. Young Josh, his face tear-streaked, school forgotten, stood, white and scared, beside his mother.

Serious or not, something was needed to snap Hiatt out of his confusion, or Tammy would never be found. That was plain to Longmire. He thought wryly: *Hiatt doesn't like me much anyway after last night, and he'll likely not want me helping. But*

I can make him mad enough to start his brains to working.

He said: "Hiatt, you wouldn't hunt a strayed horse like you're hunting Tammy. And a horse is bigger. Why don't you simmer down and use your head?"

Hiatt glared, turned beet-red. "Why don't you mind your own damned business?"

Longmire shrugged, reined his horse around.

Mrs. Hiatt said timidly: "Josh, he's only trying to help."

Hiatt grunted sourly: "Sorry, Lyman."

Longmire murmured—"All right."—and waited.

Now Hiatt's good sense and real ability began to take over. He called his riders in, his voice rolling across the field like the bellow of a bull. Then he put a man to riding each irrigation ditch, a couple to riding upcountry in the creek bottom, another two to riding downcountry. This way he covered all of the obvious hiding places in the valley.

Longmire, still waiting, drew Hiatt's glowering scowl. Mrs. Hiatt lifted a worried eye at the thin film of cloud that had, in the last hour, spread across the sky. There was stillness in the air, hot and oppressive stillness. She said concernedly: "Josh, there's a storm coming." She pointed to the smoke rolling from the house chimney, smoke that did not rise, but lay along the ground, still and heavy.

Longmire asked: "Has Tammy got any special

places he likes to go? Does he get up on the hill-sides much?"

Hiatt seemed to unbend a little, and with anger gone from his eyes Longmire could see the pain there, the fear. "That's the trouble. He ain't never been out of the valley. If he ain't around close, I'm damned if I know where to look."

Longmire felt a stir of pity for the man. He said: "Water isn't deep enough in the creek to hurt him. Don't worry, man."

"Don't worry?" Hiatt almost roared the words. "You ever lose . . . ?" He quieted abruptly and mumbled: "Sorry."

Mrs. Hiatt began to cry.

Time dragged, and in the Hiatts terror mounted. Wind breathed out of the north, hot at first, gradually chilling. Hiatt's riders came in, empty-handed, and Hiatt's face turned gray.

Mrs. Hiatt shivered, as Hiatt tersely organized the men to search the hillsides across the road.

"We'll spread out, far enough apart to do some good, but close enough so's each man can see the ones on both sides of him. We'll work back up the hillside as far as the timber goes, then we'll swing and come back to the road. The rest of you keep quiet. I'll do the calling. Tammy'll answer me, if he hears me." Hiatt scowled darkly, and Longmire knew he was adding the mental reservation: *If he's able to answer.*

Hiatt and his riders moved away, with Hiatt

grumbling: "Wish I had them three men I left up above Lyman's place last night."

Longmire offered: "Want me to get them for you?"

Hiatt hesitated. He seemed on the point of agreeing, but at last he shook his head. "Not yet. Not yet, anyhow."

"Le Clair wouldn't take advantage of a situation like this."

"The hell he wouldn't! Wouldn't surprise me none if. . . ." He shook his head. "No, I reckon that ain't quite fair."

But Longmire was wondering. Le Clair would know that once he got his sheep safely through Longmire's place, and into the upper valley, that the likelihood of trouble would be sharply reduced. With Hiatt's riders busy hunting a lost boy. . . .

Mrs. Hiatt, pitifully small, terribly helpless, stood at the gate, watching, twisting a scrap of handkerchief in her thin hands. She called: "Josh, you'll let me know? You'll let me know right away?"

"If I find him, I'll fire three shots."

Longmire turned and spurred his horse down-country, into the creek bottom. He supposed that Le Clair had ridden out of the country, had headed into Utah after his gunman, Chet Swann. But this was too damned pat, Tammy's disappearance just at this time when Hiatt needed all of his riders to hold Le Clair's sheep out of the upper valley.

Wind increased in velocity and now moaned coldly through the trees and brush that lined the creek. Concern touched Longmire, for he knew that this was to be one of those wet, cold, unseasonal storms that can hit the high country in spring with but a few short hours' notice. Tammy had to be found, and within the next couple of hours, or he might be found too late.

His respect for Hiatt had grown in the last few hours. Never before had Longmire seen other but the arrogant, blustering side of the cowman. Too, Longmire himself, although reluctantly, had wondered if Le Clair had not stolen Tammy, yet Hiatt had been unwilling, even in his agitated state of mind, to believe such a thing of his neighbor.

An odd situation, but not exactly a new one. Hiatt and Le Clair had lived as neighbors for as many years as the country had been settled, had ridden together, worked together. Yet they would fight as bitterly and fiercely as strangers over the grass of the upper valley.

Longmire rode openly out of the creek bottom and into Le Clair's yard.

Thin plumes of smoke lifted from the tin chimneys atop both bunkhouse and ranch house, to be whipped instantly away by the howling, cold wind.

Longmire yelled: "Le Clair! Hello, the house!"

The house door opened, the bunkhouse door as well, almost simultaneously. Le Clair stood framed in the kitchen door, pipe in mouth, his woolen shirt sleeves rolled up to his elbows.

Longmire said: "Thought you went to Utah."

Le Clair shook his head, frowning. "Rode as far as the railroad. Sent off a telegraph message."

"You seen Tammy Hiatt? He's lost."

Le Clair came out. Longmire was watching his face closely, and its plain astonishment could not have been feigned.

Le Clair shivered. "They better find the tyke. It's getting cold. How long's he been gone?"

"Since daybreak, I guess. A kid can walk a long ways in three hours."

"By golly, yes." Le Clair lifted his voice toward the bunkhouse. The wind snatched the words from his lips. "Beany! Joe! Schwartz! Saddle up. Hiatt's lost his boy. We'll go help him look."

The crew filed out of the bunkhouse, slipping on jackets, and headed for the corral. Mrs. Le Clair came to the doorway, a dark, stern-faced woman in her early forties. She screeched across the yard at Le Clair.

"Hector, you hitch up the buckboard. I'll go up and sit with Missus Hiatt."

Longmire rode close to the corral fence and spoke over it. "When does Swann arrive?" He could not keep the cynicism out of his voice.

"Tonight." Le Clair made his reply off-handedly, in much the same tone as he would have used had Swann been just another new rider.

Longmire felt like saying: *You'll help Hiatt today, and try to kill him tomorrow.* But he held his tongue, seeing at last that Le Clair did not really anticipate a fight. Le Clair was running a bluff.

For an instant, the impulse was strong in Longmire to laugh. The next instant he wondered what he could possibly have to laugh about. Le Clair was supremely sure that the name, Chet Swann, would put Hiatt's tail between his legs, would make him run.

But Longmire was equally sure that he had judged Hiatt right in guessing that Hiatt would never be bluffed. Not even when he knew he faced certain death.

VII

"The Truce Is Over"

Fate's inevitability dogged Longmire as he watched Le Clair and Le Clair's three cowpunchers ride up the lane toward the road. Waiting, while the three cowpunchers had saddled horses, while they dragged the old buckboard out of the barn and hitched it up, Longmire had briefly talked to Le Clair, had briefly skirted what he knew to be a touchy subject.

"What the devil do you want to bring sheep into the country for? Why not stick to cattle?"

Le Clair had grinned uncertainly and shrugged expressively. "I do not know the cattle. I have them, and I live from them, but I do not get rich like Hiatt does. He knows the cattle. I know the sheep. I can take the sheep and get rich like Hiatt does."

A simple enough explanation, Longmire now admitted. But he'd asked: "What makes you think Hiatt will back away from Swann?"

Another grin, another expressive shrug. "I would back away from Swann. Any man with sense would back away from him. Hiatt is a man with sense."

Longmire had thought: *You underestimate Hiatt. He's got sense, but he's got temper, too . . . and more damned stubbornness than you could ever understand.* Now he hesitated briefly between the downcountry course, wanting to see Edie, and a return to Hiatts' to assist in the search. There had never been any real choice, he admitted as, shivering, he put his horse into the wind. Tammy had to be found. One man more or less would probably make no difference, but if Le Clair could help, then Longmire sure as hell could.

Riding, anxious for this to be over, he put his mind to thinking of the boy, and wondered what would attract a four-year-old on a bright spring morning. Deer on a hillside—a rabbit in a field—a school of bright minnows in the creek. He thought: *Boys and water. Boys and mud. Boys and boats.*

Downcreek. He'd ridden as far as Le Clair's yard in the creekbed. But a kid could wander for miles, following a floating stick, paddling in cold, clear water.

Pure impulse made him come around. Galloping, he went back through Le Clair's yard and took a southward course downcreek.

Nearly two miles of uncultivated sagebrush scrub stretched between Le Clair's lower fence and Sheridan's upper one. Tiny, sharp flakes of snow pelted against Longmire's back. Before he had reached Sheridan's fence, the air was thick with them, and they increased their size until it seemed that they were cold, dripping blankets that could cover the ground entirely in a matter of minutes.

The creek rippled along, now between white banks, and Longmire knew how frantic must be the Hiatts by now, how terrified the small, cold boy, wherever he was. Longmire himself wished that he had worn a coat this morning. Yet who could predict these sudden storms of spring?

He dropped the gate in Sheridan's fence and rode through. In the utter silence as he put it back up, he suddenly heard a thin, small cry.

Imagination, he told himself, yet he knew it was not.

He yelled: "Tammy! Tammy, sing out!"

The cry again, and Longmire was running. He scooped the wet and pallid child into his arms. He ran back to his horse. The boy had cried himself out. His face was almost blue with cold. His eyes were big, filled with pain and terror.

Longmire mounted clumsily, and the horse began to buck down the stream, filled with fear at the unaccustomed burden his rider carried. Longmire, holding reins and child with one hand, brought a clubbed fist down viciously between the animal's ears. His left hand was iron, bringing the startled horse's head up, holding it there.

The horse quieted, and Longmire let him run out his fear. He came, this way, into Sheridan's yard and reined up before the house. Edie Sheridan came out of the door, startled and instantly compassionate, and he handed the boy down to her.

"Hiatt's youngest. He's been lost." To Frank

Sheridan he said: "Loan me a coat. I'll ride up and tell Hiatt he's all right."

The boy was safe, and would soon be warm and comfortable. Hiatt would have the news as soon as Longmire could carry it to him.

And tonight, Swann would arrive, Swann would arrive and the trouble-induced truce would be over. Tomorrow Chet Swann would ride the valley road with sudden death at his side.

Hiatt and Le Clair were at the house when Longmire rode in. The snow had almost stopped. The hillside across from the house was dotted with the dark, blurred shapes of the weary searchers. Mrs. Hiatt had a huge coffee pot on the hot stove, and her eyes were red from crying. Mrs. Le Clair was putting food into a gunny sack.

Longmire stamped his feet heavily on the porch, and stepped in through the open door. He said: "He's all right. He's down at Sheridan's, and Edie is taking care of him."

Hiatt and Le Clair were both soaked to the skin. The two had come in but a few moments before to get food and coffee for the searching riders.

Tough, arrogant, intolerant Josh Hiatt breathed a hoarse—"Thank God!"—and dropped his glance quickly and furtively to his boots.

But he had not dropped his glance quickly enough for Longmire had seen the moisture in the man's eyes. Embarrassment flooded through him, as though he had intruded upon another's privacy.

Hiatt, without lifting his face, said: "Le Clair, step out the door and fire three shots." He dabbed at his eyes with a coarse, muddy sleeve. Then he looked at Longmire. "You find him?"

Longmire nodded.

"I'm obliged. Man, I'm obliged."

"Sure."

Hiatt got up and went over to his wife. Mrs. Hiatt was sobbing with relief, her weeping wild and unrestrained.

Hiatt said softly: "Nothing to cry about now, I reckon. Let's go get him."

Outside, three quickly levered shots banged flatly across the valley. Up on the hillside, Longmire could hear a hoarse yipping, and the searchers spurred down the slope, recklessly sliding in and out of the patchy timber.

Mrs. Le Clair said: "Use our buckboard. It is already hitched up. I'll wait until you get back."

Le Clair grinned widely. "Sure . . . sure Mamma and me will wait for you. You get the boy now."

Longmire watched the Hiatts as they whirled up the lane in the rickety buckboard. He swung up into saddle. Le Clair stepped toward him.

"That boy was pretty cold, I'll bet." Relief's let-down was as plain in him as it had been in the Hiatts.

"Yeah. He was cold. I don't think he's hurt any. Scared." He thought a moment, his long mouth serious. "You're bound to put those sheep on that grass up there, I suppose?"

He thought there might have been a little shame in Le Clair's eyes, but he may have been mistaken. He knew there was defiance. "It is my grass."

"Sure. It's your grass. Hiatt's your friend, too."

"Hiatt will not be hurt. The sheep will not hurt his cattle."

"I ain't thinking about that. I'm thinking about Swann. I'm thinking about Swann and Hiatt. You got them both figured wrong, Le Clair."

Le Clair said stubbornly: "It is my grass. It is my right to say whether I want sheep or whether I want cattle."

Longmire shrugged. "Even if men get killed?"

Le Clair raised eyes that were black and surly, filled with unbending stubbornness. "Even if men get killed," he whispered through lips that hardly moved.

Longmire grew suddenly angry. "You damned fool, you don't make sense! You'll bring your crew up here today to help Hiatt because he's in trouble. But he ain't in no trouble at all today compared to the trouble he's going to be in when Swann gets here tomorrow!"

"There will be no trouble. Hiatt will not draw a gun against Chet Swann."

Longmire scowled. He stared at Le Clair and the Basque stared back unflinchingly. Longmire shrugged finally, saying softly: "I wish I had your confidence."

He kicked his horse, whirled, and galloped up the lane, the lane in which two inches of rapidly thawing snow lay. Stored warmth in the ground was thawing the snow, but the wind had turned icy.

A kind of panic was growing in Longmire, a kind of cold panic that he could not shrug away. Cursing bitterly beneath his breath, he touched the horse's dripping sides with his spurs, and at the road turned south.

VIII

"Gunslick's Return"

Alex Longmire rode hard. He pushed the horse beyond the limits of safety on the slippery road. Not yet had he put into thought the thing that was really troubling him. He knew only that he had failed with Le Clair. He must not fail with Hiatt. He must reach Sheridan's before Hiatt left. He had to have time to talk to the man.

Flinging gobs of sticky mud behind, his horse galloped into the lane at Sheridan's. The buckboard stood closely beside the house, the horse feeding from a forkful of hay Sheridan had evidently thrown down for him. Longmire knocked on the kitchen door. Edie answered it, smiling, yet beneath her smile was evidence of recent strain.

Longmire asked: "How's the boy?"

"All right now. Come in." She held the door for him.

He held back. "I'd like to talk to Hiatt before he leaves. Will you ask him to come out?"

"Of course. Is something wrong?"

Longmire had not realized that his face must be as grim as his thoughts. He forced a smile. "No."

Edie was unconvinced, but she nodded faintly. "I'll get him."

The expression she'd shown him was unsettling

to Longmire. It had been almost as though he could see her weighing him, weighing that grim expression against the things he had told her last night.

He put his back to the door and kicked angrily at a snow-covered rock. He swore silently. He heard the door open behind him, heard it close.

Hiatt asked—"You want to see me?"—with an odd inflection in his voice.

"Uhn-huh. Why don't you and Le Clair back off a ways from each other? You pull together pretty good when one of you is in trouble. Why don't you try pulling together now? You're both in trouble. Bad trouble."

"If you mean that damned Frenchman's sheep. . . ." Anger rose in Hiatt's voice, the old arrogance.

Longmire asked wearily: "You ever see Chet Swann draw a gun?"

"No."

Longmire looked at him. Hiatt's expression said: *One man. One man against ten. He won't draw his damned gun.*

Longmire said softly, almost musingly: "He's fast. He's so damned fast you don't even see his hand move. He can kill three of your men before you know what he's doing. And he'll have Le Clair and Le Clair's three riders to back him."

Hiatt spoke heavily, making an obvious effort to muffle his rising anger. "I'm obliged for your finding Tammy. I'm obliged, or I'd tell you to mind your own damned business. I won't do it, Lyman. I won't let Le Clair run sheep in the valley."

Desperation touched Longmire. Hiatt's jaw was set; his eyes were stone.

Longmire said: "You owe me something for finding your boy. If it weren't for me, the kid would have died, for you'd never have hunted him this far down."

Hiatt's eyes widened.

Longmire said stonily: "I want you to pay off. I want you to back off from Le Clair."

The panic that had been growing in Longmire all afternoon had at last put itself into tangible form in his brain. He stared at Hiatt, unflinching, demanding, unbending.

Hiatt's great hands fisted. Veins stood out on his forehead. He roared: "No! No, damn you!"

"The boy ain't worth it?"

Longmire sensed the gathering of Hiatt's body. He sensed it and started to step away. But he was too late. Hiatt's great fist exploded against his jaw, and he went back, back into the mud, into the melting snow. Groggily he sat up.

Hiatt spoke slowly, softly, but with terrible emphasis: "That was a cheap trick. I don't bargain with my family." He turned back into the house.

On his back in the mud, pride stirred in Longmire, pride and consuming fury. This was the old feeling, the feeling that took you through all the preliminaries, and turned to ice the instant your hand moved toward your gun.

He stood up, and tried to brush the mud and snow from his clothes. His fury was slow in cooling, until he looked at the house and thought of Edie. Hastily he turned his back on the house. He hoped she had not looked out the door, had not peered out the window and seen his face. Abruptly as it had come, the fury was gone.

Longmire grinned shamefacedly. He slogged through the mud to the barn and went inside. The grin faded. He had failed.

He kept telling himself: *Hiatt isn't worth it—neither is Le Clair*. But he knew he lied. He knew that their only fault was their unbending stubbornness, and he knew that wasn't enough for a man to die for. He knew as well that the loyalty of the men who rode for both Hiatt and Le Clair would not save their lives when they faced each other's guns tomorrow.

For the first time since he had crawled away from the Mill Iron's gutted line camp, he again saw the inevitable trail ahead of him. His voice was almost a cry: "No!" Desperately he tried to picture Edie in his mind. Desperately, for only she could save him.

And he failed. Edie was only a faceless blur in his thoughts, and Longmire knew he was lost.

Filled with bitterness he walked across the yard to his horse. Without looking back, he rode out of the yard and took the long, cold road toward home.

He kept telling himself: *I don't owe them anything! I don't owe Hiatt or Le Clair, either. If they want to fight and kill each other, that's their business and not mine.*

Yet he could not believe himself. He knew surely that it was within his power to prevent killing tomorrow. He knew that he could prevent it, knew that if he did not. . . .

How could he live out his life in this country with the remnants of Hiatt's family and Le Clair's, knowing that but for his own selfishness both families could be whole? How could he watch Hiatt's boys growing up fatherless?

Briefly he thought: *It's Edie's choice, too.* But there was no ring of truth to his thought. What right had he to shift the burden of decision upon Edie, to shift the guilt to her if the decision was to be staying out of the quarrel?

The miles rolled behind, unnoticed by his tortured consciousness. He rode up to his small cabin at last and entered. As though in a daze, he kindled a fire in the stove, shucked out of the wet, borrowed jacket. He went to the bed, and from beneath it dragged out his weathered and dusty blanket roll. He unwrapped it carefully and lifted out the twin Colt revolvers, the heavy, shell-hung belts.

Cold, and deadly, and smooth. They nestled against his thighs as though they belonged there, as though they now completed this man who had been only half a man before.

Longmire laughed harshly. Half a man. That was what he now was, what he would be until the last inevitable bullet had been fired.

The 700-mile trail had been in vain. The gutted Mill Iron line camp had not been the end of the trail, but only an incident along it. The months lived like a wolf in a rim-rock cave, the other months when he had lived peacefully as Art Lyman, Edie Sheridan and the fulfillment of last night—all these things were fantasy. The reality was these two guns, the trail that twisted ahead through the years, the trail that stretched, stark and naked, behind, the back trail.

In early darkness a couple of Hiatt's riders went past, trailing a pack horse, undoubtedly loaded with provisions and extra blankets for the three guards above Longmire's fence. Half an hour later they returned and in their dimly heard voices as they passed Longmire thought he could detect an almost boyish excitement.

He set the coffee pot on the stove and, when the water boiled, threw in a handful of coffee. When the grounds had settled, he poured himself a cup, and sat down at the table to drink it.

He looked around at the bare walls of the cabin. Edie would have made it look less bare, would have made it look like home. He shrugged. He finished the last bitter dregs of the coffee and stood up.

A year had passed, a year since he had handled his guns. Chet Swann had been handling his every day. There was a gap there that had to be bridged tonight.

Longmire ejected the shells from his guns and slid them back into their holsters. Then, with vast and untiring patience, he set about regaining all his lost skill. It was well past midnight before, finally satisfied, he lay down upon the bed, fully dressed.

During the night, a warm south wind breathed up the valley, and it was to the *drip-drip* of snow water from the eaves of the cabin that Longmire awoke. The sun poked its round, brass face over the rim, and laid the full warmth of its glow upon the steaming land.

Below Longmire's lower fence, Le Clair's dogs and herders brought the sheep down off the hillside, to bunch them in the bottom preparatory to the drive through Longmire's gate, waiting only the arrival of the fabulous Chet Swann.

Hiatt and his six riders came past as Longmire was eating his breakfast, riding through silently, for now upon them, perhaps, was the realization that death waited for them only minutes away. Longmire gulped the last of his coffee and rose.

He buckled on the .45s, and adjusted them so that they sat, snug and ready, at his thighs. He withdrew the guns, loaded them, and seated them again in their holsters easily, loosely. He jammed his hat down over his unruly hair.

He did not want to kill Chet Swann. The old intensity, the old confidence was not with him this morning, and he realized that this was the first time he had deliberately sought a quarrel. He would give Swann his chance, for Swann had known him in days past. Swann might perhaps recognize him and turn away. For this he hoped.

He went out to the corral and saddled his horse. He mounted, not bothering to raise the guns on his thighs, for the mounted draw. He would face Swann on his feet, for he did not know this horse. Gunfire, unaccustomed and sudden from the animal's back, might well startle him into an instant frenzy of fear, might spell Longmire's death.

With no apparent hurry or concern, Longmire rode south toward his gate, toward the gap in the fence through which the sheep must come. Yet within him was boiling all of the old cold uncertainty, that lone evidence of fear that would disappear the instant the time came to draw.

He could hear the low, steady murmur of bleating from the flock, the occasional bark of a dog. He heard a shout, heavy with Gallic accent, from one of the herders. He heard Le Clair's deep voice: "All right! Bring 'em through!"

Then he was at the gate, facing Le Clair, Le

Clair's Beany, Joe, and Schwartz, facing that other one, that one with the seamed and leathery face, the scrawny neck below it—facing those odd gray eyes that were so completely passionless.

Longmire dismounted instantly, yanked his horse around, and slapped his rump, sending him away.

He said: "Le Clair, turn around. I've bought myself a stack of chips."

Swann, unsmiling, asked Le Clair: "Who's this?"

Le Clair opened his mouth to speak, but Longmire spoke before him. "You know me. Longmire. Alex Longmire."

"Hell, he's dead. Nobody's seen him since Purvis was killed."

Longmire shook his head. "Look close. I got burned badly in the cabin with Purvis. My hair grew in differently. There are scars on my face. But I'm Alex Longmire."

IX

"Duel in the Sun"

Oddly Longmire could feel no animosity for Swann. Swann dismounted carefully, without apparent concern. He was older than Longmire, old for a gunman. He was nearly forty. His seamed face was like tanned leather. Below his not too prominent chin his Adam's apple was protruding. His shoulders were narrow, his body slight. He wore a soiled black broadcloth suit and a tan Stetson.

Nothing was prepossessing about him until you saw his guns. They branded him instantly by the way they hung, by their cleanly oiled precision. Tools of a trade, kept shining and sharp by a skillful artisan.

The eyes and the guns, equally passionless.

Longmire said softly: "Since you're La Clair's man, I reckon that makes me Hiatt's. You want to ride back down the road?" He could see that Swann was considering this by the look in the man's gray eyes.

Swann shook his head. "I guess not. My kind doesn't live long after we start backing away."

Longmire shrugged. There had never been any real hope in him that Swann would quit. He said: "Wait a minute." Without removing his eyes from

Swann, he spoke to Le Clair. "If you or any of your men draw a gun, I'll kill you first. I can do that before Swann can get me. You understand that?"

From a corner of his eye he caught white-faced Le Clair's nod.

He went on: "If I kill Swann, you will either turn around and take those damned woollies out of the country, or you'll come to a peaceable agreement with Hiatt."

Swann permitted himself a tight, small smile. "If. . . ."

Longmire shrugged. "If it goes the other way, then you've still got Hiatt to face. You think it's worth it?"

Swann stirred. His voice was edgy, and Longmire knew that his priming of nerve steadiness was wearing away. Only for a few seconds could a man stand this intolerable tension, this condition of tightly strung nerves and muscles.

Swann said: "You're a great hand for talk, Longmire."

Longmire's shoulders twitched in a brief shrug. At this instant, Swann moved. So smooth, so precise were his lightning movements, that Longmire's eyes involuntarily widened. Swann was good. Maybe he was the best.

Yet instantly the doubt was gone. Reflex, not conscious prompting, started Longmire's own right hand toward his gun. Smooth and swift, a blur of flesh and bone.

Swann's gray eyes were glittering beds of concentration. Always these things seemed to take an eternity, giving a man time to see so many things. Actually it was the tightly drawn condition of nerve and brain that made these impressions so bright, so sharp and clear. Man reached his utmost efficiency in a deadly split second, and then. . . .

Swann's gun came clear, and its gleaming blue barrel was raised. The hammer was back, the finger tight against the trigger.

But Longmire's gun was faster, almost as though it had been in his hand from the beginning. There was the briefest instant when Longmire saw death in Swann's eyes. No time for muscular reaction, no time for a widening of the lids, a shrinking of the pupil. No. He was looking directly into the man's brain through the windows of his eyes. He saw death in Swann's gray eyes, and then the smoke bellowed out from the muzzle of his gun.

His bullet entered Swann's chest, just to the left of the pocket. It kicked a puff of dust from the coat. It threw Swann's gun out of line, the barest fraction, just as it exploded. But the trigger had been pulled by a man already dead.

Longmire did not move. Yet his eyes ranged over Le Clair and his three, wild and cold, before Swann completed his limp collapse.

Le Clair yelled: "No!" Stark fear showed in his eyes, stark fear and amazement, and the next instant the old combination of fear and respect and revulsion that Longmire knew so well.

Longmire's voice was a whip. He could hear the pound of Hiatt's riders coming up behind him. "Has this settled anything? Would it have settled anything if you had shot it out with Hiatt, and a dozen men lay there instead of one?"

"Oh, God! You're right! I do not think there will be any killing, but I am wrong. I take the sheep out." Trembling, Le Clair turned to shout his orders.

Hiatt's riders yanked to a halt behind Longmire.

Longmire said sharply—"Wait!"—and Le Clair stopped.

Longmire said to Hiatt: "Do you think you could sleep good if that was Le Clair there instead of Swann?" His anger began to mount. "I got sick of killing. I put away my guns." He shrugged, as though this did not matter so much as that these two men should come to an agreement. "Le Clair ain't any more wrong than you are, Hiatt. A man ought to be able to say how he wants to make his living. There's room up there for sheep and cattle, too. Or do you want some more men spraddled out on the ground like this one?"

The bluster was gone from Hiatt. His face was pale and he could not tear his eyes from the body of Swann. "We could figure it out, Le Clair," he said. "I guess we could figure something out."

"Sure." Le Clair tried a shaky smile.

Longmire turned, caught his horse, and stalked

toward his cabin, almost dazedly. He dropped the reins at the door and went in. He sat down at the table and stared before him.

Eight. The pause in the trail was past now. The pause was past and he had better start riding. He stood up wearily and went back out to his horse.

Down the road. Down the long road to its inevitable end. He went on, past Hiatt's, past Le Clair's, almost past Sheridan's. But that would not be fair. He reined in reluctantly, grateful at least that news had not preceded him.

Edie opened the door for him, her face showing her puzzlement at his strange actions of last night. Then she saw his guns. She saw the bitterness in his eyes, the brutal bitterness.

Frank Sheridan stood in the inside kitchen doorway, watching. Longmire shifted uneasily. His hands were in the way, and he clasped them behind him. He tried to smile at her and could not.

Edie cried: "Darling, something's wrong! What is it? Come in the house."

She stepped back from the door, but Longmire shook his head.

He said: "Le Clair brought a gunman in from Utah to ram his sheep on through my place into the upper valley. Hiatt was going to fight. I stepped in and made it my fight. The gunman's dead. I killed him."

Edie's eyes widened with shock—for just an instant. Then her lips firmed with defense of him.

Longmire said: "I could have stayed out of it, but I didn't. Now it's known who I am."

He could see the turmoil in the girl plainly enough. Shock at his revelation that he had just finished killing a man had at first been paramount. Her love for him and her loyalty fought against it. Yet she still did not fully understand.

"Why didn't you stay out of it? Why?"

"Hiatt and Le Clair would have fought. If I had not stepped in, there would be half a dozen dead men in the valley instead of one."

This was the straw her loyal heart had been grasping for.

"Then you did right! You did just right!"

Tightness caught at his throat. She stood close to him, waiting. Yet he could not touch her. He put his hands up, one of each side of the door, clutching the doorjamb, and his knuckles turned white.

He said: "Thank you, Edie."

Her hands crept across his chest, up to his shoulders. Her expression held her knowledge that this was not all. She murmured: "There is more. What is it?"

Mind sickness flooded him. "I've got to go away. There is never any peace for a man who lives by his guns, never any peace for those around him."

"I'll go away with you, where you're not known." At last she saw what he was trying to tell her, and a kind of desperate terror was born in her eyes.

"There's no getting away! There's no getting away anywhere! Don't you see? The word will go out that I've killed Chet Swann. Swann was pretty well known . . . he was one of the best. Maybe he had friends. But most of them will be after me because I'm a name to add to the list that makes their reputation. It's no good, Edie. It's no good."

"But they won't find you. We'll hide!"

"No place is big enough to hide a man forever. I won't ask you to spend your life running and hiding. I won't ask you to spend it in daily terror that someone will be faster than I am."

"You don't want me," she moaned, pitifully clutching the rags of pride about her. She took a backward step.

His face settled into a deeper pattern of bitterness. "No, not that way." Seeing her face, he wished suddenly, desperately, that it had been he instead of Swann who had fallen this morning. He said, because he could not stand her stricken eyes: "It isn't only the other gunmen, Edie. They're bad enough, but mostly they let each other alone. It's the would-be gunmen, the men who have never killed before, who are the most dangerous. Don't you see? You're forever afraid to sit with your back to a door. Every time you pass a dark corner, you expect a shot out of the darkness. You're not even safe in bed. Every kid with a gun is your enemy, so long as you're able to walk and hold a gun."

"Darling, I don't care! Let me have what I can of you. Let me have that at least."

Frank Sheridan came forward at last, having heard all that was said, having seen the anguish, the weakening resolve in Longmire.

"He's right, Edie. I wish to God he weren't, but he is."

Longmire's eyes went to him gratefully. He said: "Edie, I won't drag you around from dirty town to dirtier one, from shack to hotel room, hungry and cold half the time, and then leave you alone, probably when you need me the most."

"Stop it! Stop it! You can't talk me out of being in love with you! You can't talk me into forgetting. . . ."

Longmire looked over her head, into Frank Sheridan's eyes. He said harshly: "Hold onto her, Frank."

Her eyes were tear-filled, loving, hating, stricken. Sheridan pushed himself away from the kitchen table and put his hands out toward Edie.

Suddenly Longmire saw something desperate and completely mad in Edie's eyes. She was staring with horrified fascination at his hand. His right hand. Before he could move, she seized the heavy door and with all her strength it shut, pushing, pushing, releasing a little and pushing again.

Pain, more terrible than he had ever known shot up Longmire's arm from his hand, his good right hand, caught on the hinge side between door and jamb. Pain that clouded his vision, that made his brain reel. Anger and madness raged through his mind. He flung himself against the door and it burst inward, throwing Edie to the floor, but releasing the crushed and bleeding hand.

She was wholly still on the floor, her eyes wide with horror at what she had done. Pain can make a man rage, but the rage in Longmire quieted at the sight of her tortured face. He looked at his hand, crushed almost flat across the knuckles from the terrific pressure and leverage. Splintered bone stuck through the flesh.

And then Edie's eyes dulled, filled with tears of utter hopelessness. Her voice was the merest whisper. "Oh, darling! What have I done to you? I thought I was helping. I couldn't bear to see you go!"

Frank Sheridan said quietly: "She's trying to say that no one can make a reputation by killing a gunman who can't use a gun. She's trying to say that now they'll let you alone."

Blood dripped from the hand, the only sound in the room save for Longmire's heavy breathing. Wildness still lived in his eyes. His mind, so filled with pain, was slow in comprehending words.

Sheridan said: "You hate her for what she's done to you, but you ought to thank God that a woman can love you that much."

Longmire shook his head. "I couldn't hate Edie."

Nausea turned him faint. He went to the chair and sat down. Edie sprang up, ran to the stove, and poured a pan of hot water. Her face was dead-white, her lips almost blue.

She knelt before him, making soft woman cries, almost animal sounds of hurt and sympathy. She murmured: "You don't have to go now. You can stay here. If you can't shoot, they'll let you alone." She began to tremble. "Can you ever forgive me for what I've done to you?"

Longmire managed a small smile. He felt a wonderful, soaring gladness. He tipped up her chin with his good left hand and said: "It's all right, Edie. I'd trade the whole arm for you."

The pan clattered at Longmire's feet. And Edie's face was hard-pressed against his chest. The woman fragrance of her rose to his nostrils, and for this wild, sweet moment, all pain was gone.

His Swift and Deadly Gun Hand

I
"Steep and Narrow Trails"

They were married in the town of Bend, twenty miles east along Grand River. Ruby O'Connell was radiantly beautiful as she stood beside him with an occasional glance at his smashed and bandaged hand.

Floyd Coleman didn't show it, but fear knotted his belly every time he thought about that hand. Apparently it was easy for Ruby and her father to believe that a man's past could be erased and his future assured by the mere act of smashing his swift and deadly gun hand. But Coleman was afraid it would take more than that. Men have long memories where death is concerned. Old man Sloan wasn't likely to forget that it was Coleman who had fired the fatal bullet into Will Sloan, his son.

Sloan wouldn't forget. Neither would he consider Coleman's smashed hand when the time came for Coleman to face him.

Coleman knew suddenly that in spite of what Ruby and her father thought, the time would come when he'd have to face Sloan again. The more incredible a story was, the faster it traveled. And Coleman's story was truly incredible, from the 700-mile flight out of Wyoming, to the burning

Spade line camp. From the shallow grave inside the Spade cabin where Moody had buried him alive so that Sloan couldn't find him, to Moody's death, with a score of bullets in him.

Again Coleman could almost smell the acrid smoke, could almost feel the cool dirt against his burned face, could recall his panic as he tried to draw breath through the rusty tin can that Moody had put over his mouth and nose and left protruding from the ground so that he could breathe.

He remembered the months that had followed, the unending pain of the slow-healing burns. He remembered the astonishment the first time he had seen his stubble of hair growing back in—white.

And he remembered his soaring joy as he realized he no longer looked like Floyd Coleman, that he could now take a new identity and leave the past behind.

Rockwell had spoiled that, Rockwell and Lamont. Lamont had brought in Slick Mercer, had hired Slick Mercer's gun to drive a wedge for sheep in the upper valley. There'd have been a lot of dead men in the valley if Coleman hadn't stepped in. But Coleman had faced Mercer and killed him. Peace reigned in the valley because he had. Now Coleman's identity was no longer a secret.

He heard the minister's voice drone on, reciting the marriage service. He felt Ruby's light, soft hand on his arm. He looked down at her, his eyes tender.

Courage. Ruby had all of that a woman needed. What other woman could smash a door on the hand of the man she loved, not to hurt him but to keep him from following again the gunman trail?

Coleman tried to look ahead, tried to ignore that back trail along which would come Sloan as inevitably as death itself. Coleman tried to feel the faith and belief in the future that Ruby's calm and happy expression showed. He failed, and knew he failed.

He knew as well that he must never let Ruby see his doubt. She must have these next few months with no shadows to darken them. Coleman had tried to leave to spare Ruby heartbreak. Now, he must try to shelter her from his own doubt.

The little church was crowded. Rockwell was here with his wife and two sons. Lamont with his wife and most of his crew. The remainder of the church was taken up by the river valley folks, by the residents of the town of Bend.

Coleman heard their whispers throughout the service. He could imagine their words, indistinguishable from where he stood. They would be telling each other: "That's Floyd Coleman. Fastest gunman that ever lived for my money. He beat Slick Mercer the other day. Killed him. Now his hand's smashed. Ruby O'Connell done that. She figured nobody'd try an' kill a gunman with a smashed hand. But me, I don't know. Plenty of punks don't care how they build up a name, just so's they build it. An' mebbe Coleman's purty near as good with his left hand as he is with his right."

The minister said: "I, therefore, pronounce you man and wife."

Coleman looked down at Ruby. Her eyes were bright with happy, unshed tears. He gathered her into his arms, lowered his mouth to hers. An envelope of privacy surrounded them for an instant. A whole new world opened up to Coleman. He whispered: "My wife. My own wife."

Then there was the backslapping, the congratulations, the demands for a chance to kiss the bride. He and Ruby ran out of the church with rice pelting them from behind, from both sides. He helped her up onto the buckboard seat and unwound the reins. Tin cans tied to the rear axle bounced noisily along the ground as he pulled away, scaring the horses and making them run. Laughter and shouted good wishes drowned out the noise.

The frightened, running horses scared Ruby, and she threw her arms around Floyd. Or maybe she wasn't scared at all. Maybe she just wanted her arms around him. He wanted that, too. Forever.

At the edge of town, he pulled the horses in, brought them to a plunging halt. Handing the reins to Ruby, he got down and cut loose the string of cans.

Driving again, Coleman frowned. Would Sloan let him alone now, or would he make that 700-mile trek from Wyoming again? How great was the man's hatred, his desire for revenge? Was it a normal man's hatred that could cool and die with time, or was it an obsession that would grow with the passage of years?

Only time could answer that. Coleman drove with his left hand. His right, still bandaged, throbbed as he flexed it. Doc Olsen had said he could use it again—for working—never again for gunfighting. Coleman knew gunmen who had been left-handed. Good ones. But he didn't know any that had changed hands after they got started.

Coleman himself had never used his left hand to shoot with, only to change guns when the right one ran out of cartridges.

Ruby murmured worriedly: "You're so solemn. What are you thinking about?"

He smiled and drew the horses in. He looped the reins around his wrist and put his arms around her. He said: "I was wishing we were home already. I'm an impatient man."

She blushed, but her glance didn't waver. "I'm impatient, too, Floyd."

Grinning, with Sloan forgotten, Coleman turned his attention to the horses.

The sun went down long before they reached home. In soft, gray dusk, Coleman drove up the valley road. He drew in the lane at O'Connell's, so that Ruby could get her things. While she went through the house, making sure she had left nothing that she would need, Coleman stood on the porch, staring moodily downcountry. He couldn't account for this somber mood he was in. This was his wedding night. He ought to be happy, untroubled.

It was Sloan that kept bothering him. He couldn't forget the implacable way Sloan had followed him and Moody all the way from Wyoming. He couldn't forget the vicious, vindictive way Sloan and his crew had pumped bullets into Moody's body, long after Al was dead.

He heard a racket of hoofs on the road, a shout—the crowd, heading upcreek to shivaree him and Ruby. They'd beaten him home.

But they didn't pass by. They turned in the lane at O'Connell's and came thundering toward the house. An odd silence about them struck Coleman. They weren't whooping and shouting the way a shivaree crowd ought to. They were silent, intent. And there were no women among them.

Automatically Coleman's hand dropped to his side. He wore no guns today. He would wear no guns ever again. He felt naked and defenseless. Suddenly a new thought occurred to him. Perhaps this crowd was not composed of his friends at all. Perhaps it was Sloan.

Inside the house, Ruby blew out the lamp and came to the door. She touched Coleman's arm and whispered: "Don't let them know we're here."

"They saw the lamp." Coleman felt tense, really scared. His lack of guns might stop some men from killing him. It wouldn't stop Sloan. Sloan could shoot Coleman down in cold blood and feel good about it afterward.

He considered the matter of time in his mind as the crowd thundered through the inside gate. Had there been time for the news of Coleman's survival to travel north to Wyoming, for Sloan to gather a crowd and come this far? He nodded almost imperceptibly. It had been three weeks since the shooting with Mercer. Time for his hand almost to heal. Time for telegraph messages to go out, for newspapers to print the news that a gunman was alive, that he had killed again. Time, if the news were spread that way, for Sloan to learn of it and make the 700-mile journey south.

Barely time, if Sloan wasted none. And Coleman knew suddenly that he would waste none. Coleman knew now surely that he had been a fool. Ruby had been a fool and so had her father. There was no escape from the past. Not for a man like Coleman. Not for a gunfighter.

But it was Lamont's quick, Gallic voice that came out of the plunging press of horseflesh in the yard. "Coleman! Is that you?"

"Yeah."

"Who's with you?"

"Ruby, of course. Who else?"

"I've got bad news."

Ruby gasped and her small hand tightened on his arm. A great emptiness began to grow in the pit of Coleman's stomach. It stayed for the space of a dozen heartbeats and then anger began to replace it.

Lamont said: "Man looking for you in Bend this afternoon. Man with half a dozen riders with him. Name of Sloan."

Ruby's face was white in the near darkness. "Darling, what is it?"

Coleman said harshly: "He wants to kill me. He'll never rest until he does."

Lamont, astride his horse in the darkness, said: "Floyd, I reckon us in the valley here owe . . ."— his voice broke, but he swallowed and went on— "owe you a hand with Sloan. We'll back you up, won't we, Rockwell?"

"Blame' right. Don't let it throw you, boy." Rockwell's voice was gruff.

All right. Here was the way out. Ruby's body made a soft, fragrant pressure against his side. He could feel her trembling. He could buy his life and his freedom at the price of one or more of the lives of these men facing him in the yard. He had revealed his identity for the sake of saving lives here in the valley. Now let them return the favor. Let them use their own lives to buy his.

Sloan could be defeated. He had but himself and his men. Lamont had a crew of five. Rockwell had seven. With Coleman, that would make fifteen.

Double Sloan's force. Sloan would die, and perhaps two or three of his crew. A couple would die in this bunch. But Coleman could live—could go on with Ruby.

A high price—too high. Coleman knew he couldn't go on living, knowing his life had been purchased with half a dozen others.

He said: "No. Loan me a horse, somebody."

Ruby pulled him around to face her. She said: "Floyd, what are you doing?"

"Pulling out. Is there another way?" His voice was bitter. "I was afraid you were being too hopeful. I let myself believe what you believed because I wanted to. But it's no good. Sloan won't rest until I'm dead. The only thing that will stop him is his own death."

Ruby's voice was bitter, cold, as she gestured toward the men in the yard. "They will help you."

"Sure," he said brutally. "If you want me at the cost of two or three of them."

Rockwell dismounted and came toward the porch. "Take my horse. He's the best in this bunch."

"Thanks." Ruby had stepped back. Coleman caught her arms. But she was stiff, resisting. She said incredulously: "You're my husband! You married me! Do you want me to believe that you're leaving?"

"Ruby, please." He was begging, begging for her understanding.

But she said in the same cold voice: "You want to go! You're sorry you married me and you want to go! Sloan is only the excuse."

"Ruby, that isn't it." He was growing desperate, for he was beginning to see that she'd never understand, that no woman could understand this. "Ruby, tell me good bye. I'll be back, as soon as I can."

She shook his hands from her arms. For a long moment she was utterly silent. Then she said: "No. Don't come back. Don't ever come back." She whirled and ran into the house. He heard the sofa creak as she threw herself upon it. He heard her muffled sobs.

He took a swift step toward the door, but then he stopped. If he went in there, he'd stay. He'd stay and face Sloan with Rockwell and Lamont behind him.

Decisions were easier for women to make. They didn't look into the future the way a man did. They didn't weigh costs against obligations. But Coleman knew, if he bought his own life with the lives of his friends, Ruby would eventually hate and despise him for it, just as he would despise himself.

Shrugging wearily, he turned away from the door. She'd get over it. She'd recover. O'Connell could get the marriage annulled since it had never been consummated. And Ruby could go on from there.

Coleman unwound the bandages from his injured hand. It was still scabbed across the knuckles. It was pale in the early darkness. He wadded the bandage up and threw it away. Then he took the reins of Rockwell's horse. "I'll leave him in the corral at my place."

Rockwell grunted: "Good luck, man."

"Thanks." Coleman swung to his saddle and turned the horse. He rode up the lane. Behind him, all was silent.

He knew how these men were feeling. They were blaming themselves because they had not insisted on helping him. But keeping them from insisting was their fear of death, their sense of responsibility to their families.

He raked the horse with his spurs and kept him at a fairly steady run. Time was running out. Coleman no longer had a gunfighter's certainty in his own ability. He was as helpless as a lamb among a pack of wolves. Yet he had the reputation of a wolf. Let someone call him, anyone, and he would be a dead man.

Where could he go? Where, in all this vast land, was a place that a crippled gunman could go to build up his strength and his skill, where he could sleep without having to watch his back? Where was there a place where he could think and figure and decide on his course before he was forced to kill again, or before he was killed himself?

He reached his own cabin. Hastily he buckled on

the guns, checking them for load, tying them down on his thighs. He crammed a sack full of grub. He got the buckskin bag of gold coins from under his mattress, poured the money into his palm, and counted it: $108. Ruby would get the ranch, if she'd take it. If she wouldn't, Frank O'Connell would see that it was looked after.

Coleman stared around at the cabin. But for Sloan's arrival, he and Ruby would be beginning their married life here tonight. Now it was over.

Hatred for Sloan and Sloan's kind soared like a flame through Coleman's brain. Why couldn't they let him alone? Why couldn't they let a man be? He'd put away his guns, determined to die himself before he would kill again. But when the showdown came, his determination had wavered. No man can deliberately sacrifice himself. Coleman guessed that, after all, self-preservation was man's strongest, most powerful instinct.

Couple that instinct with man's reasoning power, and you were left with but two courses in a case like his—flight or fight. Coleman couldn't fight alone, and he wouldn't ask for help.

He took a final, wistful look at the cabin, then he blew out the lamp and trudged outside, lugging the gunny sack of grub. He unsaddled Rockwell's horse and loosed him in the corral. He mounted his own horse and rode out into the pasture to drive in the others.

He would go west, and, where he was headed,

horses were money. Besides his saddle animal, he had three. He haltered them all, tied the lead rope of the second to the tail of the first, the lead rope of the third to the tail of the second. Holding the first one's halter rope, he mounted and turned west.

The method was the fastest for a man who had to travel steep and narrow trails, fastest for a man on the dodge.

He splashed through the creek and climbed slowly upward through the cedars and oak brush. An old Indian trail climbed up across the steep slide and zigzagged through the rim. It took Coleman forty minutes to make it from the valley floor to the top of the rim.

Somber and sad, he stared downward toward the cabin he had just abandoned. And then he saw the light, a pinpoint flicker from one of the windows. It grew rapidly until flames leaped from the smashed and open windows, made a blazing square of the door. The light of the flames silhouetted the tiny figures of horsemen in the yard.

Sloan hadn't wasted any time. Coleman had tonight, and that was all.

II

"Twin Guns"

When Ruby O'Connell—Ruby Coleman now—came outside, Rockwell and Lamont and their riders were gone. There was nothing but emptiness in Ruby now. It was hard to believe that no more than an hour ago her life had been rich and bountiful and full of promise. She surveyed the wreckage, still-faced, remembering her words: "Don't come back. Don't ever come back."

Had she meant those words? She didn't know. Foremost in her thoughts was Coleman's anxiety to be gone. She could remember the story he had told her of the scrape that had put Sloan on his trail. She went over it in her mind.

Coleman had the faculty of making things seem very real as he told them. He had made Ruby see the Wyoming saloon, the sawdust on the floor, the polished brass spittoons. A poker game going over in the corner, the bar lined with a payday crowd of cowpunchers.

Coleman, riding through, had simply stopped with Moody for a drink. Nothing wrong with that.

Will Sloan, just turned twenty, sneered at the twin guns that both Moody and Coleman wore. Sneered and scoffed contemptuously. To Coleman it had been a pattern he recognized. A gun-carrying kid, big with the weight of the vast ranch his father owned. A kid with enough whiskey in him to make him reckless, foolhardy.

Coleman had downed his drink, angered, but not enough to fight. Coleman had known he could easily kill Sloan. But Coleman didn't like killing. He avoided it by turning his back, by stalking away.

He'd had no choice. Ruby could admit that. He'd had no choice if he were telling the truth. Moody's shoulder drove him aside, making Sloan's treacherous first shot miss. As he fell aside, Coleman's gun came out and up with its lightning, magical speed. His first shot killed Will Sloan before he could fire again. His second took the bartender in the shoulder, even as the man poked a shotgun muzzle above the bar. Moody killed Sloan's foreman, who, out of loyalty, had drawn his own gun.

There had been sincerity in Coleman as he told Ruby the story that could not be doubted.

But to old man Sloan there was no wrong in the fight but Coleman's and Moody's. The old man's sun rose and set in Will Sloan. He had been heir to a vast domain, and the old man had lived for him and for nothing else. He had gathered a bunch of his cowpunchers and come after Coleman and Moody, and he had killed Moody at the old Spade line-camp cabin.

Coleman had escaped because of Moody's crazy

idea that he should bury himself in the burning cabin. Moody had overturned the table atop the shallow grave. And after Sloan and his crew had left, Coleman had dug himself out.

Ruby's thoughts were interrupted by the drum of hoofs on the road. Half a dozen riders turned at the lane and came pounding up to the house. This would be Sloan, Ruby knew. She could feel her face paling. A middle-aged man leaped from his horse, and the animal set his hind hoofs and skidded to a halt. Sloan came around the animal's head, and strode toward Ruby. Darkness had come down, but Ruby still wore her white wedding gown and was obviously visible to the man.

He said harshly: "Where is he?"

"Who?"

"Damn you, don't play games with me. Coleman. Where is he?" The man seized her arms roughly. His fingers were like talons, and Ruby gasped with pain.

Ruby was silent. Sloan flung her away from him.

She sprawled on the porch floor, tearing her dress. He stood looking down at her, just for a moment. Then he strode into the house. He found a lantern in the kitchen and lighted it. He came back out onto the porch.

In lantern light, Ruby could see him. He was a big man, broad of shoulder, thick of chest. His hair was gray and coarse. A paunch made him seem spindly-legged and top-heavy. He wore a long, curving mustache above his cruel, thin-lipped mouth. His eyes were blue bits of ice in a dark-tanned face. He bellowed: "Sands, come get this lantern. Take it up to the road and find out which way he turned when he left here."

A cowpuncher dismounted and walked to the porch. He took the lantern and moved away. Sloan looked down at Ruby, who was now getting up, angered at last. He said: "So you married him."

"Yes." He made no move to help her up, and she could feel the contempt in his whiplash voice. Outrage began to burn in her. She said sharply: "Yes, I married him. The neighbors wanted to help him fight you. I wanted him to accept their help. But he wouldn't do it. Do you know why?"

"He's yellow," Sloan sneered. "All these damned killers are yellow. That's why he ran."

"No. That wasn't it at all. If you knew him, you'd know that wasn't why. He's sick of killing. Can you believe that? He didn't want to see any more men die because of that smart kid you called your son."

Sloan hit her. A back-handed, open-handed blow that popped like a pistol shot in the night silence. Ruby fell back against the wall, dazed. She murmured: "If I had a gun, I'd kill you myself."

"Sure you would, you she-wolf." He laughed. "But you ain't got a gun, have you?"

The cowpuncher with the lantern came back at a trot. Sloan swung to his saddle. The cowpuncher said: "He turned upcountry. He's headed for his own place. Mebbe we can beat him to it if we hurry." The cowpuncher flung the lantern to the ground. It smashed and went out. The men spurred their horses and whirled up the lane. And in a few moments, the night was still again.

Ruby sat down on the top step, trembling. She began to cry. She had known a murderous anger, had directed it at Sloan. She realized that, if she had had a gun, she'd have killed him, or tried at least. The knowledge both surprised and shocked her. Never had her emotions reached such an intensity before.

The patient *clop-clop* of a trotting horse reached her ears. This was her father, returning from Bend, driving the buggy. She saw the shadowy bulk of the buggy come along the lane, and she ran out to meet it. She tried to keep a grip on herself, but as Frank O'Connell climbed down with an exclamation of concern, she flew to his arms, crying unrestrainedly.

"Ruby, what's the matter? Where's Floyd?"

"Gone! He's gone!" She knew she had to control herself. Sobbing this way, she would never get the story out. She stepped away from her father, forcing herself to be calm. O'Connell's voice was deep, compassionate. "Ruby, what's happened?"

"We'd just arrived here to get my things. Rockwell and Lamont rode in and told Floyd a man named Sloan was looking for him. This

Sloan's crazy, Dad. He hit me and knocked me down."

O'Connell was a quiet man, a peaceful man, but now his voice was strange. "Ruby, go to the house. Go to bed. I'll do what I can." He did not wait to see if she would comply. Swiftly he unhooked the buggy horse and led him away. A few moments later, he rode out of the corral, running, on a fresh and saddled horse. Ruby called to him, but he paid no attention, and rode up the lane without a backward glance. Ruby screamed—"Dad! Dad, come back!"—but she got no answer.

She turned toward the house. There was fear in her now. She knew sending her father after Sloan had been foolish. She stopped, hesitating. Then she ran into the house.

Frantically she tore her wedding dress off. She snatched a split skirt from the closet and stepped into it. She kicked off her slippers and put on her boots. A man's shirt completed her dress, and, as she went out, she snatched up a buckskin jacket.

There were no fresh horses in the corral, only the buggy horse, tired from the trip to Bend and back today. She saddled him swiftly and swung up. Quirting the animal, she ran out of the yard and took the road that led upcountry toward the place that was to have been her home and Coleman's.

Frank O'Connell rode hard. He gave his horse no rest at all, no respite. The animal began to sweat and a light froth formed over his glossy hide. Still O'Connell ran him.

He did not know exactly how much start Sloan had. Fifteen minutes, perhaps. But Sloan's horses were tired, tired from the hard ride getting to Bend.

Sloan and his men had passed O'Connell in the buggy after he had left the river, sweeping past grimly with neither a hail nor a wave. Frank had wondered about them then.

He was realizing now that Ruby had made a mistake in smashing Coleman's right hand in the door. She should have let him ride out the day he killed Mercer. Now she was married and her husband gone, perhaps already dead. Frank O'Connell scowled.

What kind of a man was this Sloan? he asked himself. What kind of man could hit a woman decked out in her wedding dress? Logic answered. The same kind who could make a career of trailing a man that had killed only in self-defense. Sloan.

At least Coleman knew he was being pursued. With a crippled right hand and a clumsy left, he could not defend himself against them. But he could run. And he could shoot a rifle.

On impulse, Frank rode in at Lamont's, circled the yard, shouting: "Ride after me! Coleman needs some help." He rode out again without slacking his pace, but behind him he could hear shouting, confusion. He could see lamps suddenly glowing out from doors hastily flung open.

He rode in and out at Rockwell's the same way. Five minutes behind him, he knew, would come a dozen galloping men. What he hoped to accomplish, he didn't know. But the more he thought of Ruby, the madder he got. They'd not treat his girl that way and get away with it. Not if he could help it.

The miles flowed behind, torturingly slow. The horse he rode began to falter. He reached Coleman's wire gate, slowed to be sure it was open before he plunged through. At the house, he pulled to a halt just as the first glow of fire began to light its interior.

Sloan grabbed the bridle of O'Connell's horse. "What the hell do you want?"

"What are you doing? Burning him out? Did you catch him?"

"Not yet." Sloan laughed. "But we will."

"But the fire. Why that?"

"Accident." Sloan laughed again. O'Connell caught the strong smell of coal oil. He said: "Liar."

Sloan's powerful hands pulled him from his horse, dropped him as he cleared the saddle. O'Connell hit the ground, sprawled out. Sloan kicked him in the ribs. Pain laced through O'Connell's thin body, pain and quick-kindled rage. He got up. He didn't wear a gun, but there was a rifle on his saddle, snugly in the boot.

He backed against the horse, felt the gun boot prodding his back. He let a hand slip around. He

113

said: "I wondered about Coleman. I even doubted the story he told about you. It was hard to believe that a man like you existed. Now I know he told the truth. I'm going to take you into Bend to the sheriff, Sloan. For burning Coleman's house. For assaulting my daughter."

He whirled then, snatching the rifle out of the boot. Sloan was taken largely by surprise. O'Connell jacked a cartridge into the chamber.

Sloan's gun cleared leather, cocked. Its muzzle lifted as O'Connell closed the action on the Winchester. Before O'Connell could curl his finger around the trigger, Sloan fired.

The bullet took O'Connell's leg out from under him, boring through the fleshy part of his thigh. He fell back under the hoofs of his horse. The horse jumped away. The rifle had fallen from O'Connell's grasp.

Light, reddish-yellow, came from the blazing house. O'Connell looked up at Sloan, surprised, with the anger driven out of him by the pain of his wound. His eyes widened at what he saw. Sloan was crazed with rage. He was leveling the gun in his hand at O'Connell's head. O'Connell stared, amazed. He yelled: "No! For God's sake, man!"

Lust for vengeance had driven all humanity out of Sloan. His finger tightened on the trigger, and the gun in his hand roared and bucked. A small hole appeared in the center of O'Connell's forehead, and he fell back against the ground, instantly dead. An expression of utter amazement remained on his face, in his widened eyes for a moment, and then it was gone. . . .

Sloan must have heard Rockwell's and Lamont's riders coming. Because when they arrived, Sloan and his men were gone. All that was left to show for their presence was the blazing cabin—and Frank O'Connell's body.

Rockwell picked up the rifle and jacked it open. He smelled the barrel, scowling. Ruby came pounding into the yard. Rockwell said gruffly, anxiously: "Lamont, get her. Stop her before she sees him."

But he was too late. Ruby flung herself from her horse. Her face was very pale as she knelt beside her father's body. She stared, dry-eyed. Rockwell clumsily lifted her to her feet, turned her toward him, and pulled her face against his chest.

She did not cry. She did not tremble. She was steady and still, shocked beyond comprehension. The fire in the cabin popped and crackled. Its heat seared the men standing in a circle around Rockwell and Ruby.

At last Ruby pulled away, her face drawn, filled with pain. She asked in a voice that was scarcely audible: "Floyd? Did they get him or did he get away?"

"He got away, honey. He got away."

Determination hardened the girl's eyes, stiffened

the expression on her face. "Then I've got to find him. Because he's the only one who can help me now."

"Honey, he can't do anything. Sloan's after him, too."

"He can kill Sloan," she whispered. "And then he can come back to me."

III

"Not from the Law"

Coleman traveled all through the night. Morning found him off the plateau, riding along the bank of Grand River, heading ever west. He avoided contact with humans, detouring all the towns he passed. All day he rode across the broad reaches of desert. At pauses for meals he turned his horses loose, all but one, and rotated the one he rode at each stop. The miles fell behind.

At intervals, Coleman would glimpse lava or shale beds in the distance, and he always availed himself of the opportunity thus presented. He would detour five miles to cross hardpan, shale, or lava bed. And he always came out of these places on a different course from the one by which he entered.

He laid confusion and delay along his back trail. He wandered for miles along the narrow beds of streams, and worked out elaborate schemes for coming out of the streams without leaving a too easily spotted trail.

A man got to be expert at these things. But Sloan was an expert, too, or he could not have followed Al Moody and Coleman those 700 miles without losing them.

Now, Coleman spent an hour, each morning,

noon, and night, practicing the left-handed draw. He patiently worked stiffness out of the smashed hand, but it was obvious, even from the first, that the hand would never again fire a gun with any skill or certainty.

He was, therefore, forced to a single conclusion. His gun hand, thenceforth, was to be his left, with the right taking the rôle of drawing the second gun, passing it to the left when the left-hand gun was empty.

Coleman forced himself to eat with his left hand, learned to write with it. He made it do all the things the right hand had formerly done.

Slowly he began to gain a certain degree of skill. He risked a stop at Moab for cartridges, and then traveled on south through the Ute Reservation.

He fought the viciousness, the hatred, the hopelessness that crept over him whenever he allowed himself to think of Sloan, of Ruby O'Connell. He grew thin and gaunt. But at last he convinced himself that he had shaken Sloan off his trail.

Yet he knew that Sloan, having come this far, would now hole up in some town and wait. He'd wait for news of Coleman to come over the grapevine. And when he heard it, he'd be on the move again.

In the middle of the Ute Reservation, Coleman's grub ran out. He went a day without eating, without sighting game, and then, at evening, rode into an untidy Ute village.

Most of the Indians were dressed like whites, in blue overalls, flannel shirts, and straw hats. They were incredibly dirty.

The night was mild, fragrant with desert springtime. Fires winked and smoked in the village. A pack of half-starved, scrawny dogs followed Coleman in, yapping ceaselessly at the heels of his led horses.

Squaws bent over cast-iron pots hung above the cooking fires. Children stared with wide-eyed fright. Coleman dismounted in the center of the village and waited.

The commotion quieted, but he knew all eyes were upon him. At last, a huge, fat Indian approached him. The man must have weighed over two hundred pounds. Greased braids came from each side of his head and lay across his chest, nearly reaching his waist. Like most of the others, he wore a straw hat perched squarely upon his head. The Indian raised a hand in the universal sign of greeting and spouted a stream of unintelligible Ute at Coleman.

Coleman grinned at him. He pointed to himself and said: "Coleman." He rubbed his flat belly, saying: "Hungry."

The Indian looked at him suspiciously. The Indian's eyes dropped to the two low-swung guns and lingered there. Finally he said, stabbing his chest with a dirty thumb: "Black Tail, chief."

Coleman regarded him steadily. The Indian's

glance wavered. He turned and shouted something in Ute. Then he tugged at Coleman's sleeve.

Coleman followed him. They came to the chief's lodge, which was the only one Coleman saw that utilized hides and conventional design. All the other lodges were ramshackle huts built of scrap lumber, brush, and mud. Coleman tied his saddle horse to a stake and followed the Indian inside.

A fire burned in the center of the floor, the smoke rising to the peak of the teepee. A fat squaw tended a pot on the fire. A child was sleeping on a pallet at one side of the lodge. Coleman sat down when the Indian indicated where he was to sit.

An idea was beginning to stir in Coleman. He knew how close-mouthed Indians were. He could hide out for months here in this village or near it, and the chances were good that not a word of it would leak out. Yet he had no Ute language, and it was fairly obvious that no one here knew English.

The squaw served him a tin plate of meat stew. The brave produced a brown bottle of whiskey. Coleman ate and drank gratefully. When the squaw refilled his plate, he ate that, too. The whiskey put a warm glow of well-being within him.

When the meal was over, the Ute produced a pipe, filled it, and handed it to Coleman. Coleman smoked the acrid tobacco in silence. At last the Ute spoke, and Coleman's eyes widened with surprise. The Ute said: "You trade horse?"

Coleman nodded, grinning. This one was a sly

fox. He had waited to reveal his knowledge of English, had waited to see if Coleman would let anything slip. Coleman grunted: "Maybe."

"You run from the white man's law?"

Again Coleman grinned. "Not from the law. From many men who would like to kill me."

"The Ute Reservation is small, but it is large enough to hide a man."

Coleman said nothing. He waited. Finally the Ute said: "Black Tail likes your spotted mare."

Coleman nodded thoughtfully. "She's a good animal. She can run like the wind. She will give you many fine colts." He watched the desire leap high in the Indian's dark eyes. He said: "I give her to you. In return, you will give me food and show me where a man may camp and not be found."

The Ute nodded, trying unsuccessfully to hide his satisfaction. Coleman withdrew one of his guns. He looked at it thoughtfully. He said: "If I am found, you will die. Is it understood?"

"It is understood."

Coleman got up and went outside. The spotted mare was the last in his line of horses. He untied her from the horse in front and handed the halter rope to the Ute chief. He mounted his saddle animal, and untied his grub sack. He handed it down to the Ute. Black Tail shouted a stream of Ute words that sounded like imprecations. Squaws came running and took the sack. Black Tail ducked back into his teepee and returned with the bottle of

121

whiskey. When the squaws came back with the filled sack, the Ute laid the bottle inside and handed up the sack to Coleman.

Coleman tied it behind him. Black Tail mounted the spotted mare and led out into the darkness.

This land went by the name "desert", yet it was not desert at all. Grass grew everywhere, along with low and scrubby sage. Water was scarce, yet a man could always find water within an hour's ride. Badlands and weird rock formations reared themselves above the level flatness of the plain at intervals, displaying colors ranging from green to deep red. It was to one of these rocky badlands areas that Black Tail led Coleman.

After about half an hour of threading through the scattered rocks, he came to a narrow valley shaded by willows that were more bushes than trees. A stream wandered down through the valley, making a whispering, melodious sound.

Black Tail did not even dismount. He stopped, turned, and said: "Stay here." Then he rode away.

Coleman got down. He was tired, sleepy. Yet it seemed to him that all this had been too easy. Probably Black Tail was only pretending friendship. Later, when Coleman was sleeping, he would return with half a dozen of his braves. Coleman still had three horses, probably a little gold, and the two fine Colt's revolvers he wore at his waist, to say nothing of the Winchester in the boot on his saddle. In a lonely place such as this, it was

122

unlikely that his body would ever be found. When it was, no one could trace his murder to Black Tail.

Coleman grinned. He tied his saddle horse in a clump of willows, off-saddled, and rubbed the animal's sweating back with the saddle blanket. He released the other two horses, and they moved slowly away, grazing.

Since Coleman had already eaten, he did not bother with the sack of grub, other than to get the whiskey and take a long pull at it. He built up a fire. He cut brush and fashioned with it what would appear to be a sleeping man. He covered this with one of his blankets. At its head, he put his saddle, and arranged his hat on the saddle so that it would look as though he had placed it over his eyes to keep out the glare of the fire.

He stood back then, looking down at his handiwork with approval. He decided that even to the eyes of an Indian his creation looked like a sleeping man if not viewed from closer than fifty feet away.

Satisfied, he retreated up the hillside and found himself a niche in the rocks where he could remain hidden. He lay down and pulled the second blanket over him. He jacked a shell into the hammer of his rifle and leaned it up against a rock. Then he went to sleep.

It was a faculty all men developed sooner or later if they lived on the trail. Sleep came quickly when they lay down. It disappeared just as quickly when something happened to wake them.

When Coleman finally did awake, his eyes went quickly and automatically to the skies. The stars told him it was near morning. Probably three-thirty or four. He tried to place with his mind the slight noise that had awakened him, failing. The noise had been too faint, too small to engrave itself on his memory. Yet he knew he had heard it. He knew Black Tail had returned.

Without stirring, he watched the embers of the fire, the dark blob on the ground nearby that was supposed to represent him. He watched for a good fifteen minutes before his eyes picked out a creeping shadow in the gloom.

Carefully he eased the gun from his left hand holster. The rifle was useless in this light. With the revolver, Coleman knew he could shoot by feel.

Killing. They forced it on a man whether he wanted it or not. In this case, the prod was Black Tail's greed. Coleman thought of Ruby, and wondered why he did.

Instead, then, of the easy way, flinging a shot at the creeping Indian, Coleman waited. The Indian closed the distance between him and the form by the fire, then with a sudden, rushing leap eliminated it altogether.

Coleman laughed aloud. He made his laughter strong and mocking. He said: "Black Tail is not only a fool. He is also a thief."

The Indian had leaped to his feet immediately, realizing as soon almost as he dived that he had been duped. Now, he crouched, ready to flee. Coleman's voice was sharp. "Don't move. I can kill you before you take a step."

The Ute straightened. Coleman could not be sure, but he thought it was the bulky, fat form of Black Tail. He said: "Call in your braves."

The Ute chief spoke a short sentence in his own language. Three shadowy forms converged upon him, and stood, silently waiting.

Still Coleman lay, unmoving. He said: "The others, too."

Black Tail spoke again, and two more braves came to stand beside him. Coleman laughed again. He said: "Get out of here. And if you come again, come by daylight."

He watched the Indians melt away into the darkness. Then he put his head down and slept.

The days passed uneventfully. Coleman spent them perfecting his skill with his left hand. He was fortunate enough to kill an antelope and finally, by the time both it and his other grub were gone, decided he was as good with that left hand as he would ever be. While his speed with it could not match the speed he'd known with his right hand, he thought it would keep him alive. So, one day he mounted and headed south.

It was time to face whatever he had to face. A man couldn't hide forever.

IV

"Tough Town"

Again he was on the move. Leisurely, now, he traveled southward through Monticello, Dove Creek, and Cortez. He forsook the high country north and east of Cortez for the desert and dry country to the south.

He bought a new outfit at a Ute Reservation trading post in Shiprock, and traded a horse for a pack outfit and a load of grub.

All days were the same now. Spring passed, and still the solitary figure of Coleman and his led pack horse moved like specks across the vastnesses of the immense Southwest.

Although he knew he was a fool, there were times when loneliness weighed heavily upon him, and against his better judgment he would pull into a settlement, a stage relay station, or even into a solitary ranch house for the sake of company and companionship.

Tall and lean, bronzed and weathered by the sun, his white hair contrasting sharply to the mahogany of his face, he found not companionship but only nervousness, fear, and distrust in those he met. A gingham-clad woman, gazing at him as he rode in, would greet him with the words: "Water your horse and ride on. Trouble's cheap and easy to find hereabouts."

A town marshal would appraise him as he passed the jail, and then turn back inside avidly to scan his Wanted notices. He'd catch a town bully measuring him as he stood at the bar somewhere, and he'd turn and get out because staying would mean a gunfight as soon as the bully worked up his courage to the point of challenge.

Coleman carried the stamp of wildness, from his lean, armed thighs, to the bright alertness of his eyes. Men, to him, became not men at all, but only problems to be studied and solved in the interests of self-preservation. They were not fellowmen to Coleman because they would not allow themselves to be. He gained their awe without trying. He knew he could never gain their friendship as long as the two guns rode his thighs. Yet, because of Sloan, the guns stayed.

He began to hate Sloan with a corrosive and consuming intensity. As the days passed, it began to seem incomprehensible that he had ever run from the man at all. Now, the only thing he desired was a meeting with Sloan. Death might be the outcome. Yet he knew he could take Sloan along, and that would be enough.

Nights, staring at the limitless bowl of star-studded velvet above him, he would think of Ruby. He would wonder if she were still his wife. Thinking of her in another man's house, in another man's arms, was torture of the most exquisite kind.

To avoid this torture, he formed the habit of

going back over his life. He would take each man who had fallen before his guns, and he would think: *I could have stopped it there.* Then he would recall the way that particular fight had shaped up, and he would blame himself because he had not found a way out of it without killing.

It was mental self-torture, until his mind was exhausted and he could sleep. But his conclusions were always the same. Each time he had killed, he had only acted in self-defense. Backing down, being cowardly, might have saved his life part of the time. It would not have saved it forever. There was but one thing he had done wrong, that being strapping on the gun that first time.

To some men, a gun is a tool, but to others it is an instrument of perfection. Coleman was one of these. Shooting a gun was for him as natural as pointing a finger. Skill with it had come as naturally as breathing.

Edgy as a hungry wolf, he came into Troncosa, Texas in midsummer. The town sprawled untidily on the bank of the Canadian, hot, dusty, sleepy at midday, appearing nearly deserted.

He jogged, head down, through the sparsely populated streets, until he came to an adobe building before which were racked half a dozen hip-shot horses drowsing in the blistering sun. Against the north wall in a narrow strip of shade, a dozen Mexicans snored peacefully, their hats tipped over their eyes.

Coleman looped the lead-rope of the pack horse around his saddle horn and dismounted stiffly. For a moment he stood, stretching the riding cramps out of his body. He debated a moment between the saloon and the pump next door, finally walking to the pump to soak his head in its cool, gushing stream. He took a drink from the dipper hanging on the pump, then rinsed his mouth, and spat. Dripping, he walked back and pushed through the saloon doors.

He stepped aside immediately, waiting until his eyes would become accustomed to the gloom, his hand resting on the top of a glass case. He looked the crowd over. A stout, mustached man in a broadcloth shirt stood at the end of the bar, glass in hand, watching him. At the other end, a Mexican dandy was talking with a girl. In between were three men, two of them obviously cowpunchers from some neighboring ranch. The bartender was bald and bearded. Beads of sweat glistened on the top of his head.

Over on a far wall, three men were playing cards at a table. Coleman could feel either the open or the surreptitious glances of them all upon him. He glanced down at the glass case under his hand.

His hand came away as though it rested on a hot stove. He jumped a step, starting. Automatically that left hand found the grip of his gun. Then he relaxed, grinning shamefacedly. The stout man at the end of the bar chuckled. He called: "Never see a Gila monster before?"

Coleman grinned. "Never saw one in a saloon before. Surprised me." He took a long look at the ugly little animal beneath the glass. Then he stepped over to the bar and took a place beside the stout man in the broadcloth suit.

The man stuck out a hand in the first gesture of friendliness Coleman had experienced since leaving Bend. "My name's Murphy. Len Murphy. There's a case full of rattlesnakes at the other side of the door."

Coleman looked. He could see, even from here, the dust-brown coils of a fat rattler behind the glass. "Devil of a place to keep things like that."

Murphy's grin was pleasant and easy. It was not a forced try at friendliness, but a natural one. Murphy, Coleman decided, was one of those rare creatures that like people—all people. Murphy said: "Feltzer, give him a drink."

The bartender had a smooth, sallow skin and blue eyes that bulged in their sockets. He slid a bottle across the bar to Coleman, and then a glass. Coleman poured out a stiff one. The attention accorded him as he came through the doors had dwindled, and now he could hear the soft slap of cards being dealt at the table across the room, the low, murmured conversation of the three men at the bar as they cursed heel flies and bog holes and line-camp grub and the lack of women in Troncosa.

Murphy was watching him, a faint grin on his round face. "Feltzer gets a big kick out of seein' a drunk stagger against one of them cases on his way out of here. Nine times out of ten, the drunk'll turn around and buy a couple more drinks."

Coleman, with his habit of weighing men, was trying to weigh this Murphy. There was a surface geniality about the man, but there was something else about him, too, a deeply hidden toughness that Coleman could only guess at.

Coleman was reminded that, while Murphy had introduced himself, Coleman had not. And he was tired of hiding, tired of masquerading under a false name so that Sloan couldn't trail him. He had reached the point where he would welcome Sloan and an end to running.

He said: "Coleman's my name. Floyd Coleman."

Murphy nodded. "Heard of you." He looked sheepish. "Maybe I was a little unfair." He flipped back his vest to reveal a silver star pinned to his shirt. His eyes were narrowed and sharp as he watched for Coleman's reaction.

Coleman grunted bitterly. "So now you'll hurry back to your office and run through forty or fifty dodgers, looking for me."

"Will I find you?"

"Let's go see." In Coleman's eyes was a deliberate challenge. He finished his drink. He caught Murphy studying the way he drank with his left hand.

131

Murphy looked puzzled, but he led the way out of the saloon, which was called the Llano. Sun heat rose in shimmering waves from the dusty street, distorting the view. Nothing moved, so far as the eye could see, save for the tails of the horses switching endlessly at flies that settled upon them.

The sheriff's office occupied part of a low, adobe building a block and a half from the saloon. The other half was occupied by a lawyer named Dobson. The entire rear of the building, behind both offices, housed the jail.

The sheriff kicked open the heavy plank door and led the way into his office. He settled himself in a squeaking swivel chair and waved a hand at a leather-covered sofa. Coleman sat down.

Murphy said tentatively: "Odd to see a man as young as you with white hair."

With anyone else, Coleman might have felt a stir of anger. He was puzzled that he did not. He decided the reason he didn't was that Murphy so obviously was not prying.

He said: "I'll save you some time. I'm not wanted, so far as I know, anywhere."

Murphy studied him, finally nodded. "I believe you're telling me the truth. You're runnin', though, ain't you?"

Coleman stood up. Anger stirred him, and a faint flush stained his face. The sheriff said: "Sorry." He looked so put out, so upset, that Coleman's anger couldn't help fading. The sheriff grinned at him shamefacedly, saying: "This is a tough town. You can't blame a man for wanting to know what he's up against."

Coleman sat down again. "What do you want, my life story?"

"Nope, but I'd like to know if you're going to stay around here. If you are, I'd like to know who's likely to show up lookin' for you."

Coleman stared at him. With his habit of weighing men, he seldom had much trouble putting one where he belonged. But this Murphy puzzled him. His first inclination was to discard Murphy as a garrulous fool, a friendly, ineffective figurehead of a lawman.

Yet something that didn't show on the surface troubled him. Murphy had more to him than met the eye. You caught it at times, half hidden in Murphy's eyes. You sensed it in the oddly thrifty way the sheriff moved.

Coleman said: "I'll be around for a week or two. Whoever shows up looking for me, I'll handle myself. That answer your question?"

He got up and went to the door. Murphy did not, by word or action, try to stop him, so he went out into the blazing heat of the dusty street. Over the roofs of the low buildings he could see a towering frame structure that could only be a livery barn. He got his horses and rode north. At the second intersection, he turned east.

The livery barn, a good hundred yards long,

was built upon thick adobe walls that formed its foundation.

He swung down inside the wide doors. A middle-aged Mexican came out of the cool depths of the building, and Coleman handed him the reins. "Grain 'em," he said. "Grain 'em every day. I'll be around."

"*Sí, senor.*" The hostler showed him an expanse of gleaming teeth. Coleman walked back the way he had come. He began to think of Ruby. And thought of Ruby inevitably brought thought of Sloan. He frowned. Soon now, maybe sooner than he expected, Sloan would come riding out of the north. Perhaps he would come openly and perhaps not. Coleman could realize the possibility of being taken entirely by surprise by Sloan's arrival. A call from a dim-lighted alley. A shot immediately following.

Yet Coleman could not believe that would be the pattern. Sloan had followed him too long to let that be the way of it. Sloan would want to gloat, and he would want Coleman's death to be slow and painful.

Coleman hoped he would come soon.

He walked past the Llano and went on another block to the Plains Hotel. He signed the register, and climbed the stairs wearily. All of the long miles behind were beginning to tell on him now. He lay down on the bed, fully clothed without even removing his guns, and inside of five minutes was asleep.

• • •

Days passed pleasantly for Coleman. He enjoyed taking his meals in a restaurant, enjoyed the novelty of sleeping every night in a bed. Mornings found him increasingly in the sheriff's company, for the man continued to seek him out. Afternoons, he usually took a ride to the prairie to practice with his guns. Two weeks went by.

One morning he noticed an unusual somberness about the sheriff. And the conversation took a different turn. Murphy seemed to want to talk about himself. He began to talk about St. Louis. "I was born there, you know." He stared at Coleman thoughtfully. Then, apparently deciding something in his mind, he said: "I was a pretty wild kid. Didn't have no folks. Lived off the town. I went to Oregon with a wagon train when I was fifteen. Killed a man that liked to bully me and took off across country by myself."

Murphy's eyes were reminiscent, brooding. But they kept themselves fixed on Coleman, and Coleman felt that a part of the man's concentration was reserved for him.

Murphy said: "Killed five before I was twenty." Coleman scowled. Murphy looked at him, long and hard. Finally he said: "There's only one way a man can quit, son." He pulled back his vest and displayed the star.

Coleman laughed. The sheriff puzzled him and made him uneasy. What the devil was Murphy, a

135

mind-reader? Or had he simply read the expression of brooding unhappiness in Coleman? Had he translated the bitter loneliness in Coleman as a desire to put aside the guns?

Coleman asked: "How does that help?"

"Why, I guess it's because folks don't take kindly to having their lawmen killed. Killin' one generally results in havin' another one after you."

It was something Coleman had not previously considered. His mind had probed and sought endlessly at the problem he faced, but never had it even touched upon this possibility. Yet he still didn't have the full answer. He said: "All right. But suppose someone's on your trail? Suppose he's got five or six men with him, and the only thing he wants in life is to kill you? What could you do if an outfit like that showed up, looking for you?"

Murphy looked nonplused for a moment, and finally shrugged. Coleman, staring out the window, saw a strange cavalcade come past in the street. There were six wagons in all, drawn by four horses apiece. Each wagon was piled high with rolls of wire. Coleman's thoughts were distracted momentarily from his personal problem and he asked: "What the devil? What's all the wire for?"

A glance at Murphy told him that this was Murphy's problem, just as Sloan was Coleman's. The sheriff's round face was troubled, frowning. "Big outfits are puttin' the country under fence. But there's more to it than that. Nine out of ten of the big outfits ain't got a legal claim to more'n half what they're aimin' to fence. They're fencin' in a bunch of squatters an' small cowmen. The squatters an' small cowmen don't like it. They'll probably fight."

"What for? How're the fences going to hurt them?"

Murphy grinned wryly. "It's a long story. Most of the little outfits have built up their herds by mavericking, by branding strays. Ain't no law against that. Even the big outfits do it. But some of these little guys have overstepped reason. They've registered brands that can cover almost every brand in the country. They've been re-branding the cattle belongin' to the big outfits. And they know that, as soon as the fences are finished, they're finished, too."

He fished a cigar from his pocket and bit off the end. "As soon as the fences are done, the big outfits are goin' to be able to watch their grass and their cattle like they never did before. The squatters know it'll be the end. So I reckon they'll fight."

Coleman grinned. "And you'll be in the middle. I guess I'd be worried, too, if I were you."

"Ain't worried so much. But I need help."

Coleman's expression turned wary.

Murphy went on: "I need a man that ain't acquainted hereabouts, that I know blamed well ain't mixed up with one side or the other. You interested?"

Coleman shook his head. But he was beginning to wonder.

Murphy must have seen the hesitation in him. He pressed his advantage hard. "Hundred and fifty a month."

Still Coleman shook his head.

Murphy frowned for a moment and finally said regretfully: "You get on my side of this, and I'll back you when your man comes lookin' for you."

"Back me? What d'you mean by that?"

"I mean what I say," Murphy growled testily. "I'll back you with the law or with my guns, whichever it takes."

Coleman stared at him. He stood up. "I'll think about it. I'll let you know." He tried to pierce the bland expression on the sheriff's face. He wished he knew the man's thoughts.

Murphy said: "All right?"

Coleman had his hand on the doorknob when he turned. "Which side is the sheriff's office on?"

Murphy grinned. "A good question. But I can't answer it. I'm damned if I know myself. If I said I'd try to stay with the side that was right, it still wouldn't be much of an answer. There's right on both sides, an' wrong, too. Let's say I'm in the middle, sure to be wrong whichever way I jump."

Murphy's round face was wry with self-derision. He stood up suddenly. "You eaten yet?"

Coleman shook his head.

Murphy got up and settled his hat on his head.

"Come on down to the restaurant with me, then. I'll fill you in on the whole situation while we eat."

Coleman shrugged, still puzzled by the strangeness and the abruptness of Murphy's proposition. He went out into the blazing street, and walked beside the thickening figure of the sheriff. Was the man setting him up to do a job he himself was afraid to do? Or was he sincere and honest, merely wanting a deputy who was able with his guns and who was not involved locally?

Coleman's money was gone. He had to do something; he realized that. And a job would inevitably involve him in fighting. It was one of three things, then, move on, take the sheriff's offer, or take a riding job with one of the outfits here in the Panhandle.

Moving on was out of the question. Coleman was tired of running. And if it was to be fighting, he had just as well have the hundred and fifty the sheriff offered as thirty from some cow outfit.

His mind was nearly made up when he sat down at the shaky restaurant table. But he decided he'd wait and hear it all before he finally accepted Murphy's offer.

V
"Let This Be Him!"

Riding back downcountry that night, Ruby sat straight in her saddle, straight and stiff. Her face was white, her eyes tearless still. Rockwell rode on one side of her and Lamont on the other. Behind came their crews and, farther back, Frank O'Connell's body, tied across the saddle of a led horse.

Ruby did not know exactly what she planned. She was too stunned to know. But she was sure she would not stay here. Somewhere Coleman was riding, and in him rested Ruby's hope of life and love. Without him, she knew the future would be blank and hopeless, indeed.

As they turned in at Rockwell's gate, she said: "Mister Rockwell, would you want to buy our cattle? I'll need money to hunt for him."

"You better stay here, honey. You better stay here."

"No. I'm going. He'll never come back. He'll go from one town to the next, until finally he gets tired of running. He'll turn and face Sloan then, and he'll be killed. I want him to know what Sloan's done before that time comes." She stared hard at Rockwell. "I'm going anyway, but it will help if I have some money. And I can't wait for roundup time."

Rockwell looked at her helplessly. He said gruffly: "Well, all right. I'll give you five hundred dollars. You let us know where you are, and, soon as we get the cattle tallied, I'll send you the rest. Market price at roundup time. That fair enough?"

"Of course it is." She let him help her dismount at the house. He drew Mrs. Rockwell aside and whispered out the story. Mrs. Rockwell took over at once, tiny, sharply sympathetic. Ruby undressed and sank gratefully onto the bed. Mrs. Rockwell blew out the lamp and stole silently from the room.

Ruby began to cry then. She buried her face in her pillow and cried until she was exhausted. She cried for her father, still and limp and cold on the ground, his body lighted by the unearthly orange glow from the blazing cabin. She cried for Coleman, fleeing because he would not involve the local people in his quarrel with Sloan. If he had only known that Sloan would kill her father! Then he might have stayed.

But Ruby had to admit that might have been even more disastrous than this. Besides her father, Coleman himself would now be dead. Perhaps either Rockwell or Lamont, or both of them, might also be dead.

And Ruby wavered that night, too. Wavered for the first and last time. She wondered if she would not be wiser to stay, to obtain an annulment of her marriage to Coleman. Somehow she could pick up the threads of her broken life. Coleman alone had brought this trouble to the valley.

Yet, in honesty, she had to admit that he had averted more trouble than he had brought. But for him, the valley would have been bathed in blood over Lamont and his effort to ram sheep through into the upper valley. Slick Mercer would have cut down two or three at least, probably Rockwell and O'Connell among them.

Also, Ruby came to the realization that love is not a rationalizing force. It does not weigh the good and bad and bestow itself only where there is good.

She came to the realization that she loved Coleman above all else, and that no matter what happened she had to find him. She knew she would help him with Sloan if no one else would. She knew that, when the time came, she would have the strength to kill Sloan herself if need be.

And Ruby O'Connell knew a cold and paralyzing fear that her own action in smashing Coleman's right hand might be the cause of his death before she could reach him.

Shivering, bathed with icy, sweating terror, she finally slept.

The next four days were a nightmare for her. She packed away her father's things in trunks and boxes. Her own things, the things she would need, she packed in valises that she could take with her.

142

She watched her father's body lowered into a grave on the hillside in back of the house.

Like Coleman, Ruby began to know a growing hatred for Sloan. But for him, she would now be happy with her husband. Her father would be here, here where she could see him whenever she wished.

She told herself that hatred was not the answer for her troubles, but she could not help herself. Hatred was all that sustained her.

On the day she left Bend, she went into the sheriff's office there and, with Rockwell and Lamont, swore out a warrant against Sloan, charging him with the murder of Frank O'Connell. Perhaps Sloan would never be found. Again, it was possible that this action might be the means of his eventual defeat. It was a chance that Ruby could not afford to overlook.

Carrying a copy of the warrant, she climbed into the stage and set out over the rocky, bumpy road toward the east. . . .

Days passed, grew slowly into weeks. Ruby grew thin, and her eyes took on a haunted look. She spent almost a month in Denver. She talked to every stranger she met, read every out-of-town newspaper she could find. She paid $200 out of her small and dwindling hoard to a detective agency that claimed to have offices throughout the West, only to find after the money was gone that their Denver office was their only one.

Discouraged, she journeyed south. Railroad and stage fare ate up what remained of her money by midsummer. She took a job as waitress in a hotel in Albuquerque, saving all she could from her small wages for traveling on.

Roundup time around Bend did not come until October. Ruby knew it would be late November or early December before she could expect any more money from Rockwell.

In August, a man passed through Albuquerque *en route* to Oregon from Texas. He was a short, thick-set man with ridiculously short, bowed legs. He finished his meal at the hotel, and Ruby, noticing the Mexican silver buckle on his belt, asked him if he had come up from the south.

His voice, answering, carried the soft, slurred drawl of the Southwest. "Yes, ma'am. From Texas."

"I . . . I'm looking for a man. A young man with white hair. Have you seen him?"

"I saw one like that, no more than a week past. A man who wears two guns, tied down to his legs. A bad one, ma'am."

Ruby could feel a flush of excitement rising to her face. Her hands began to tremble violently. Her knees felt as though they could no longer support her. "Where did you see him?"

The man hesitated. Ruby seized his shoulders with her two frail hands. Her fingers bit into his muscular flesh. She shook him, but it was like a terrier trying to shake a bull by the hind leg. "Where did you see him? Where?" she almost screamed.

"Why, ma'am, when a man passes through as many little hamlets as I have, they all run together in his mind." He looked at her as though he doubted her sanity. Her eyes were wide and staring, her lips parted and bloodless. She was praying frantically: *Oh Lord, let this be him! Let this man remember where he saw him!*

She forced herself to be calm. It wasn't easy. Her stomach felt as though it were a small, painful, and knotted fist. Her breath came in quick, ragged gasps. She sat down, heedless of other customers waiting to be served.

She whispered: "Think. Oh, please, think hard. He is my husband."

The man's expression softened somewhat, lost some of its startled puzzlement. He said: "Why sure, ma'am. I'll try. Let's see now, when was it I seen him? Last week about this time I was camped on the Canadian." He smiled apologetically. "I ran out of grub. I stopped and broke a couple of hosses for a man down there."

Ruby thought she could not stand this tension. She wanted to scream at this slow-talking man, make him remember, make him talk—and quickly. But she restrained herself with a visible effort.

He said: "Two weeks ago, I was crossin' the Llano. That was where I got the Injun scare." He smiled. "Comanches, ma'am. They gave me a fright for sure."

Ruby said with constrained patience: "The white-haired man. Please. Please try to remember."

"Ma'am, I reckon it was in Mobeetie. It must o' been there. I ain't sure, you understand, but it seems to me it was there that I came into this saloon. Dog-gonedest place you ever seen, ma'am. They was two glass cases in the saloon, one on each side of the door. One of 'em was full of big, fat, diamond-backs, and t'other with Gila monsters. You ever see a Gila monster, ma'am?"

Ruby was almost screaming. "Please, where is Mobeetie?"

"Texas Panhandle, ma'am. You head east outta here. . . ."

But Ruby was gone. Untying her apron, she ran through the lobby and up the stairs to her room. She knew there was a stage leaving for the east in less than an hour. She intended to be on it.

She threw her clothes into her valises with little regard for them. In ten minutes, she was packed. She carried the bags down the stairs and stopped in at the hotel office to get her pay.

"I don't want to leave this way," she said. "But I must. I've had news of my husband. A man in the dining room has seen him, he thinks in Mobeetie."

The hotelkeeper, a dry, bespectacled little man, went to the safe, and got out a small handful of coins that he handed to Ruby. "I wish you luck.

But if you don't. . . ." He smiled apologetically. "You will always have a job here."

"Thank you." Ruby smiled and took his hand. How was she going to stand the endless miles between here and Mobeetie? She had heard of Mobeetie, a wild town down in the Texas Panhandle. She did not know exactly how far it was. But it was probably close to a week's journey. A lot could happen in a week. Floyd might move on. He might be killed. But she wouldn't think of that. She'd think of the strength of his arms, of the gentleness of his smile. She'd think of the way the blood pounded through her body when he kissed her.

Carrying her valises, she walked the block and a half from the hotel to the stage depot in the blazing midday sun. It was a small adobe building. Benches stretched along both walls inside. Between the benches ran a counter. A grizzled oldster behind the counter took her money and gave her a ticket. "Stage leaves in twenty minutes, ma'am."

Ruby sat down. Beside her, a slim and pretty Mexican girl nursed a tiny baby. Across the room, a fat drummer in a black derby hat watched the Mexican girl with avid eyes. Ruby frowned. Beside that drummer sat a young cowpuncher, his sacked saddle between his feet. He was faintly flushed with embarrassment and studiously avoided looking at the young mother. Ruby stared at the cowpuncher.

Some way, he struck a chord of familiarity within her. She had seen him before. She should remember where. Perhaps in Denver, perhaps anywhere back along the miles and the months she had traveled. She shrugged and settled back on the bench to wait, forcing the tension out of her body, forcing a calmness she could not feel.

Behind the station, she could hear the high shouts and curses of the hostlers as they harnessed the stage teams.

It was beginning. With lips that scarcely moved, Ruby prayed: *Dear Lord, let me find him this time. Let him be safe and well. . . .*

VI

"I Do"

Coleman ate the hot Mexican food with relish. Long used to his own cooking on the trail, it provided a welcome change. Murphy sat across from him, eating with sober concentration. When they were finished, they sat sipping coffee, and Murphy produced a couple of black Mexican cigars. Coleman lighted up, savoring the welcome bite of the tobacco, the strong aroma of the smoke.

Murphy grinned. "Make up your mind yet?"

Coleman said: "Fill me in, first. What's happening, and what's likely to happen?"

"Well, it's a long story. There's a lot of different factors that have made the situation what it is. For one thing, most of the outfits hereabouts are enormously big. Some of 'em cover land in eight or ten counties, all in one piece. Naturally cattle drift, particularly in winter when the northers hit, and in summer when water holes go dry."

"Do they own all this land?"

"Sometimes none at all. They lease it from the state of Texas. Some of it they don't even bother to lease. They hold it by force. Well, anyway, when cattle drift, it's inevitable that some of them git lost. They go for a year or two without branding, and, after the calves are weaned, it's anybody's

149

guess who owns them. The little outfits have made use of that situation, by branding everything they can lay their hands on that don't already carry another brand."

Murphy grinned. "Four or five years ago, the big outfits started changin' hands, sold out to Eastern syndicates, and to Britishers looking for places to invest their money. You maybe can like a man that's come into the country with nothin' but his two hands and built a cattle empire. But nobody likes a syndicate, and blamed few people like British capital. You see what I'm getting at?"

Coleman shook his head.

"Well, instead of stickin' to branding stuff that's strictly maverick stuff, the little outfits have taken to branding over the big outfits' brands. They'll register a brand that can easy cover two or three of the big outfits' brands. Then they'll go to work. It's got so bad, that everybody's on edge about it. The big outfits' solution to the problem is miles of fence. That'll stop drift. It'll make it possible for them to keep a closer check on their own cattle. And it'll make it possible for them to either drive out the little outfits or watch them closer."

"And the little outfits are going to fight, is that it?" Coleman asked.

Murphy nodded. "And here I sit. There ain't a man in the country that ain't involved with one side or t'other. I need help. I need the kind of help that can use two guns and use them fast. What do you say?"

"And when it's over?" This was the important part to Coleman. If the star was to be a release from the gun, he wanted it to last.

But Murphy shrugged. "A sheriff is elected. You know that I'll keep you on as deputy as long as I'm sheriff. Beyond that, I can't promise you a blamed thing. It'll depend on how you impress the folks that cast the votes."

"I guess that's fair enough."

Murphy's eyes brightened. "You'll take it, then?"

Coleman nodded. "But I expect some support when Sloan comes. He'll have five or six men with him. There's only one thing he lives for and that's to gun me down. He won't care how he does it."

Murphy put a strong, slim hand across the table. There was no pudginess to his hand. He clasped Coleman's, and then fished in his vest pocket. He handed Coleman a nickel-plated star that said: SHERIFF'S DEPUTY, STONEHAM COUNTY, TEXAS.

Coleman stared at it thoughtfully. He had come a long way for this. He had never thought he'd see the day when he'd pin one on. A year ago, he'd have refused. Perhaps today was the first time he would even have considered it, and here it was.

Grinning ruefully, he pinned it on. He said: "I've never been an outlaw exactly, but I've lived by an outlaw's rules. I've considered every hand against me. Now I've got to change."

He found Murphy grinning back at him. "No you don't. That still holds true. Every hand is still against you, and will be until this is settled, one way or t'other."

Coleman fingered the star.

Murphy said: "Raise your right hand."

Coleman did.

Murphy said quickly, his words running together: "Do you solemnly swear to uphold the law to the best of your ability, so help you, God?"

Coleman nodded. "I do."

Murphy laid some money on the table for their dinner, and stood up. Outside, the town was beginning to empty for the *siesta* hour. From the walk in front of the restaurant Coleman could see about half a dozen riders. Several of them were clustered around the wagons loaded with wire that were stopped a block below the Llano. In the shade of a cottonwood three women in bright dresses were talking. One of them was idly twirling a parasol.

Murphy turned back toward his office. Coleman knew the sheriff would sleep for an hour and then head for the Llano. Coleman was getting used to this custom of a nap in the middle of the day. But he sometimes overslept. He crossed the street and entered the hotel. In his room he lay down on the bed. A breeze stirred the yellowed curtains at the window, and shortly he was asleep.

• • •

At sundown, the town of Troncosa began to come to life. From the short-grass country riders came by twos and threes steadily. These were the quick-shooting cowpunchers employed by the syndicates. Among them, wary and suspicious, came the small ranchers, none of whom employed more than two riders.

In early dusk Coleman awoke. For a moment he stared at the cracked ceiling. Then his hand went to his vest and fingered the nickel-plated star. He grinned wryly and swung his feet over the edge of the bed.

His face was covered with stubble. A shave, then, was first. He crossed the room to the wash basin and poured it half full of tepid water from a pitcher. He scrubbed his face and neck, and dried them on the thin towel. He adjusted his holsters and loosened the guns automatically and then opened the door. As an afterthought, perhaps from self-consciousness, he unpinned the deputy's badge and stuffed it down into a vest pocket. Then he closed his door and descended the stairs.

In the barbershop, he lay back in the chair and relaxed while the Mexican barber lathered his face. The door kept opening and closing as men came in. A bench along the wall held four men before the barber was half through shaving him.

He heard one man say gruffly: "You see them wagons, Sam?"

153

"Sure. I saw 'em." There was a brief silence. Then Sam turned slowly, indistinctly. The first man said: "They's two, three hundred miles of fence in them wagons. I wish to Christ they was at the bottom of the Canadian."

"Me, too." There was another silence, broken only by the scraping of the razor on Coleman's cheeks.

Then Sam said: "Bert, you thinkin' what I'm thinkin'?"

Bert made a low laugh. The barber finished shaving Coleman, wiped his face, and applied stinging bay rum. He whisked the towel off, and Coleman stood up. The barber said—"Next, señor."—looking at Sam.

Sam was a short, bowlegged man, somewhere between thirty and forty. His eyes were as blue as bits of china, but there was neither warmth nor friendliness in them as he looked at Coleman. He looked at Bert, an equally hard-eyed man, and then turned back to the barber. "I've changed my mind, Ramón. I'll be in later." He and Bert left the barbershop abruptly. Coleman fished a quarter from his pocket and paid the barber. He followed the two men out.

They were standing on the walk, staring downstreet at the loaded wagons, talking in low tones. Coleman paused and shaped a cigarette. He lighted it, and drew smoke gratefully into his lungs.

The street was dark now, save for the pale glow

cast over it by a sinking, low-riding crescent moon. Lights flickered from the Llano, from half a dozen other saloons along the street. Somewhere a man yelled. The tinkle of a piano came from one of the saloons, and a moment later a woman's shrill, vindictive voice was heard, cursing.

Bert and Sam looked at Coleman with plain hostility, then moved away toward the Llano.

Coleman hesitated. Here it was. Here was business for the sheriff's office. Here was taking sides before the star was a day old on his vest.

But there was no evading it, no ducking. Had it been Murphy in that barber chair, these two would never have been so indiscreet as to reveal their intentions. But it had not been Murphy. It had been Coleman, who they did not recognize, who they did not fear. Decisively he turned and moved at a rapid walk toward the sheriff's office.

VII

"Get out of Town"

The sheriff's office was dark when he arrived, but a light gleamed in the lawyer's office next door. Coleman went in.

The man at the desk was old, probably near sixty. His hair was as white as Coleman's. His face was dark and seamed with sun and weather. Coleman asked: "Seen Murphy?"

The lawyer nodded. "He rode out to the Triple X. Said he'd be back by midnight. Are you his new deputy?"

Coleman nodded, and stuck out his hand. "Coleman."

The lawyer gave him a reserved smile, but he took Coleman's hand. "Dobson," he said. "Lawyer."

Coleman was used to this reserve in those he met. They sized him up by his guns, by the wildness in his eyes, the ever-present wariness. He hated to barge into this short-grass quarrel on his own before the badge on his chest was hours old, but there seemed no other solution. If he didn't barge into it, those wagonloads of wire would wind up on the bottom of the Canadian. And that might split the country wide open, might provoke open and unrestrained warfare. He knew Murphy wouldn't want that.

He thanked Dobson, and said he was glad to have met the man, and went back outside. With purposeful strides, then, he headed downstreet toward the wagons.

The moon had sunk almost to the horizon. The street sounds continued. Somewhere a guitar strummed softly and a pleasant male voice sang in Spanish.

More riders came into town, by twos and threes. A cigar glowed redly against one of the wagon wheels, and a man was a black blob there. Coleman approached. Abruptly the cigar coal was hooded, and the man stood up. A voice called: "Wait where you are, friend!"

Coleman stopped, alert, nervous. This man was one of the wagon guards. Up near the head of the line he caught a stir of movement as a second guard approached. The man called: "Who is it, Billy?"

"Dunno, yet. Somebody."

Coleman asked: "You know a man called Sam, and another named Bert?"

"Sure. Sam Beckworth an' Bert Flynn. What about 'em?"

"They've got a plan that involves your wagons." Coleman waited.

"And who're you?"

"Coleman. Murphy's new deputy."

"Didn't know he had one. You shuck them guns, my friend, and step over here."

"Uhn-uh. I keep the guns." He could hear then a low discussion between the two men. Finally Billy said: "All right. Come on. But I got a rifle centered on you. Be careful."

Coleman walked slowly and carefully toward him. The sense of danger and alertness was finely honed in him. He asked them: "Who's this wire belong to?"

"It's a pool load. Part of it belongs to Triple X, part to YV, and part to D Cross."

"And where do Sam and Bert fit in?"

"Sam's place is about five miles from Bert's. Both are inside D Cross."

"How many guards you got? Just the two of you?"

"No. There's a couple more. They went over to the Llano for a couple of drinks."

"You better go get them."

"And leave you alone here with Jute? Uhn-uh, mister. Think again."

They didn't know him and therefore they didn't trust him. Coleman couldn't blame them for that. He said: "All right. I'll go after them. But don't go to sleep here. You're going to be jumped before long."

He turned his back and stepped away toward the Llano. Over on the far side of the street, his eye caught movement, but he didn't slack his pace, simply changed his course. He veered toward the walk, and, when he came to a well of shadow before a building, he stopped and turned.

Obviously there was no time left in which to fetch the guards from the Llano. He caught that movement again across the street, and then saw three separate and distinct forms move across the moonlighted space between two buildings. He called: "Bert, Sam! Give it up!"

His answer was a gun flash, and the thudding sound of a bullet as it tore into the building front four feet from him. Smoothly, instantly, his gun came out. His thumb curled up over the hammer and held it, half thumbed back.

He grinned. The rifle boomed from the wagons, and instantly one of the three across the street yelled with sudden pain. Coleman called—"Get out of town!"—and drew the sudden, concentrated fire of all three of their guns.

He dropped instantly to the walk. Glass tinkled behind him as one of their bullets found the window. From the Llano, a shout lifted. He glanced that way and saw men boiling out of its doors. He began to wonder what he had started. This town and this country was an armed camp. If Sam and Bert and their unknown cohort weren't gone by the time that crowd arrived. . . .

Coleman got up suddenly. He could have dropped one or more of the three from here in comparative safety. He cursed himself because he didn't. They were armed lawbreakers and he a sheriff's deputy. None in the town would censure him if he killed under these circumstances.

Someday, this reluctance to kill would be the cause of his own death.

Running, bent low, he went across the street. Both guns were out now, the right one held low, ready for the switch to the left hand when that one would be empty.

Ahead of him, a gun muzzle flared. The bullet tore a furrow in the street at his feet and the bullet ricocheted wickedly off into the night.

Coleman could see a little better now. Rapidly he fired, and his bullets tore into the building before which they stood, showering them with splinters and broken glass. Easily he shifted guns and kept up his barrage. He was running toward them, his gun spitting, while behind him and off to one side the rifles at the wagons roared repeatedly. It broke their nerve, this open charge. Coleman could have killed the three of them while he crossed the street. But when they broke, he halted and let them go, two running, the other limping between them.

They went back between the two buildings and disappeared behind one of them. Coleman punched the empties out of his guns and refilled the cylinders from his belt as he walked toward the wagons.

The one called Billy said shakily: "Mister, I guess we pegged you wrong."

Coleman grunted wryly: "All right. But round up the rest of your guards and keep watch this time, will you?"

He slipped into the shadows, avoiding the crowd as it surged around the wagons. A few moments later, he was at the bar of the Llano, a drink in his hand.

He had come into the open, which was the only thing he could have done. But the opening play of the game had marked him as a friend to the syndicates and an enemy of the squatters. It would be a hard label to get rid of. He might never get rid of it. It might still be on him when he died.

Coleman didn't underestimate these little cowmen. All of them, whether rustler or honest man, faced ruin if the fences went up, and the fight was only beginning.

VIII

"Mobeetie"

The stage rocked violently as it lurched along the rough road, across the endless miles of flat and barren land. Ruby sat beside the young mother, holding the child while the mother slept. Across from her, the cowpuncher dozed. The fat drummer kept his eyes upon her steadily, and every time she would meet his glance, he would give her an oily, ingratiating smile. Ruby felt a stir of dislike for the twentieth time that day.

The drummer was one of those possessed of a monstrous ego who believed each woman he met nurtured a secret longing for him that needed only encouragement to come into the open. Ruby shuddered slightly. How any woman . . . ?

The cowpuncher wakened and sat up, rubbing his eyes. Ruby studied him, wondering why he struck such a familiar chord in her. He looked across at her and smiled. "I'm Slim Edgerton, ma'am. I reckon we got a fur piece to travel together. It'd be nice to have somethin' to call you besides ma'am."

Had the same words come from the drummer, Ruby might have been offended, for from him the words would only have been a prelude to a bolder advance. From the cowpuncher, the words gave no offense. He was obviously just trying to be pleasant. Ruby said: "I'm Ruby Coleman."

At this instant the baby stirred in her arms and began to cry, so she did not see the sudden, startled look on Edgerton's face.

The child's mother awoke, and Ruby handed the baby over to her, then smoothed her skirt. When she looked up, the cowpuncher was staring at her strangely. He asked: "Miss, or missus?"

"Missus Coleman." The cowpuncher dropped his glance abruptly, almost guiltily. He mumbled: "Glad to know you, ma'am."

Ruby smiled. "I thought you wanted something to call me besides ma'am."

He smiled at her, but it was not the same. A new nervousness had been born in the cowpuncher. He said—"Yes ma'am, I did."—and he flushed furiously. Ruby studied him, struck again by the feeling of familiarity. But it eluded her. She said finally: "You seem so familiar to me. Haven't I seen you somewhere before?"

"Why, I don't reckon so, ma'am."

"Where are you from?"

"Wyoming. But I been gone from there a long time."

The stage thundered into a way station and stopped. Edgerton opened the door and helped Ruby out. Then he helped the Mexican mother who carried her wailing baby inside at once. The drummer, apparently having given Ruby up as too difficult, now followed the mother and child anxiously. Ruby frowned.

She stood still for a moment in the blazing sun. Edgerton had gone inside. A couple of hostlers led fresh, harnessed horses out to replace the sweated horses on the coach. The driver climbed down and looked at Ruby. "Dinner stop, ma'am. Half an hour."

"Thank you." Ruby went into the way station, which was a low adobe building plastered with mud. Pockmarks around the door testified to some old shooting battle that had taken place here, perhaps with Comanches. Inside, an Indian woman was carrying food to a long table. The Mexican girl and the drummer were already seated. Edgerton was engaged in earnest conversation with the station agent, a dour, scrawny man with a prominent Adam's apple.

Ruby took a seat next to the girl. She had no appetite, but she forced herself to eat. She was tired, bone weary. The lurching coach, swaying, bumping, tried the strength of men, strong and used to rough travel. It was doubly hard on Ruby, but even in her own misery she could feel compassion for the young mother, so stolid in her acceptance of the discomfort.

She began to eat listlessly. The cool air was pleasant in here, but she knew it would only make the outside heat more unbearable later. Discouragement and depression touched her.

Suddenly she missed her father, missed Coleman. She needed someone strong to lean upon today; she needed outside strength to draw upon.

She heard the single word—"Mobeetie."—out of the conversation between Edgerton and the station agent. Immediately then Edgerton got paper and pen from the station agent and began to write awkwardly against the wall. Ruby was faintly puzzled. The cowpuncher finished his letter, which must have been very short, sealed it in an envelope, and gave it to the agent. Had Ruby but known, the letter contained a single word *Mobeetie* and a signature *Edgerton*. It was addressed to *F.W. Sloan, General Delivery, Santa Fé, New Mexico*. It was a summons, a call. Within minutes after its delivery, men would be moving east. East toward Mobeetie, toward Coleman.

The cowpuncher came over to the table, sat down, and hastily gulped his dinner. Ruby finished, drank a glass of tepid water, and got up. She stood in the doorway, looking out. Her heart should have been singing, for somewhere ahead was reunion with Coleman. But it had been too long. There had been too much heartache, too much discouragement and disappointment in between.

Coleman and reunion with him was a dream, something that she worked incessantly toward, but which had no actual reality in her mind. Her informant had said: "Mobeetie." Yet the man had been most unsure of himself. Mobeetie had been a guess, Ruby judged. A guess that was probably incorrect. Also she knew that she could not afford to ignore any lead, no matter how doubtful. If Coleman was not in Mobeetie, perhaps someone there could tell her where he was.

The stage driver shouted, and the four passengers filed out into the afternoon heat and reluctantly climbed into the coach. The lurching and swaying began again. Bridges were a luxury not often encountered in this country, and every time the road crossed a wash or a dry streambed, it simply descended into it and climbed out on the other side.

Edgerton was silent, moody, and brooding. The fat drummer succumbed to sleep, much to Ruby's relief. The baby wailed fitfully in its mother's arms. The Mexican girl cooed at it patiently, listlessly.

Ruby closed her eyes, but she could not sleep. She kept thinking of the cool nights in Colorado, of the soft murmuring of Grand River. She saw again the towering rims, and her father, and Floyd Coleman. Deliberately forcing her thoughts from these things, she considered the puzzle of the cowpuncher, Edgerton. She was sure she had seen him before. Yet she had never been to Wyoming.

Suddenly it struck her. *Wyoming!* Wyoming was where both Coleman and Sloan had come from! Ruby's eyes came wide open, and she stared at the brooding Edgerton. Now she remembered! He'd been with Sloan that night, that night when her father had been killed. She had caught but a short glimpse of him, and she'd been upset with thought only for Coleman, for the threat that Sloan presented. That explained why she'd had such a hard time remembering.

Her intent gaze drew Edgerton's eyes. He stared at the pure hatred he saw in Ruby's eyes. Then he flushed.

She said: "You're one of Sloan's men. You're one of my father's murderers!"

He turned white. His lips thinned out. He said: "No, ma'am! I had nothin' at all to do with that!"

"Then who did it?"

He clenched his jaws stubbornly. Ruby gave him no time to reply. "That letter you wrote. Was it to Sloan?"

Edgerton nodded. He was plainly uncomfortable, plainly ashamed.

Ruby said: "And it told him to come to Mobeetie, is that it?"

Again Edgerton nodded. Ruby's voice was caustic. "How did my husband kill young Sloan? The same way Sloan killed my father?"

"No, ma'am." It was plain that Edgerton would have liked to crawl into a hole and cover himself up. But he straightened, hard-eyed and grim. "Will was quarrelsome. Just a mean kid, ma'am. He picked a fight with the wrong man and got himself killed doing it. Coleman didn't want to fight. He even turned away. But Will wouldn't let it go at that. Will had to try an' shoot him in the back."

"So you think it's right for Sloan to hunt down my husband?"

"I didn't say that. I don't think it's right at all. But I grew up at Z Bar. Sloan picked me up out of the gutter, in Denver, when I wasn't no more'n eight years old. He raised me. His fights are my fights, ma'am, whether they're right or wrong. Can't you see that?"

"No, I can't." She almost threatened Edgerton with the warrant she carried in her valise, almost, but not quite. She came to her senses in time. Nothing at all could be accomplished by trying to have this young man arrested. Sloan was the game she was after. She could eliminate every one of Sloan's men and she still would not stop Sloan. That warrant had to be saved for him alone. And he had to remain in ignorance of its existence.

Edgerton stared at his boots, acutely miserable. "I'll get off at the next stop, ma'am. I reckon you don't want to look at me."

"No, I don't."

Their conversation, the angry tone of it had aroused the drummer. He looked back and forth between them uncertainly. He licked his lips.

Ruby settled back in the corner of the seat and closed her eyes. Quiet desperation filled her. She had wanted to find Floyd, had only wanted to find him. And she had been the means of leading his enemies to him. *How long do I have?* she thought, and she calculated the time it would take for a letter to return, to Albuquerque, to Santa Fé, for Sloan to gather in his men and come east to Mobeetie. She had a week, perhaps a little less than that. A pitiful little time. *Lord, let it be enough*, she prayed silently. *Let it be enough. . . .*

IX

"One Man"

The temper of the town was ugly. In the Llano the small ranchers gathered, drinking heavily, making low-voiced threats. The hard-riding cowpunchers, the gunmen hired by the syndicates gathered at the wagons, discussing the attempt made to seize them.

Coleman stood between the two factions, wearing the star openly now. In truth, if his sympathies were with either side, they were with the squatters. Yet he had thwarted their attempt to seize and destroy the wire. In so doing, he had earned their enmity. He stood at the bar in the Llano, an untouched drink before him.

Murphy would have been able to quell the trouble once and for all. But Murphy was known. Murphy was liked for his impartiality. Coleman held them only by the threat and the efficient look of his guns.

Sam Beckworth and Bert Flynn came in, a man limping along behind them. Coleman left his drink and walked over to the glass case containing the rattlesnakes. He amused himself for a moment, poking his finger at the case, trying to get one of the snakes to strike. Apparently, though, this was an old story to the reptile. His glittering eyes simply fixed themselves on Coleman, the head following his every movement.

Sam and Bert made a nucleus for the group at the bar. They kept watching him, trying to gauge him, trying to guess how far he would go. Finally Sam apparently could stand it no longer. He called: "Deputy! Hey, deputy!"

Coleman looked up. Sam Beckworth had a small man's cockiness, stemming from a desire to assert himself and thus compensate for his lack of stature. Coleman weighed him as he approached the bar. You could never tell about these small men. They had a pride, a fierce and ungovernable pride that chose the blamedest times to rule them. You could never be sure of these short ones. You'd think you had them pegged, and you'd move along on the assumption that you did. When the showdown came, often as not, that damnable pride would upset all your calculations.

This one, this Sam Beckworth, had a narrow-set pair of blue eyes that were widened slightly now with a kind of panic. The thing shaping up was too big for him, and perhaps he realized it was too big.

He said: "We want to know where you stand in this."

Coleman smiled. Yet behind the smile was realization that anything, any small mistake could set things off. He said: "I stand where Murphy stands."

"Then go over to the sheriff's office and put your feet on the desk. Let things alone."

Coleman shook his head.

Sam said: "Then we'll. . . ."

Coleman's mind was working like lightning now. The men at the bar had fanned out, forming a semicircle around him. Sam seemed to realize he had Coleman boxed, and realization of it came to the others as Sam began to speak.

Coleman gave the thing no more time to develop. He stepped in close and caught Sam's wrist. With a violent twist, he brought Sam around, wrenching that arm, bringing it behind Sam's back, raising and twisting. Sam grunted with pain, and a muffled curse escaped his compressed lips. Coleman turned him, thus putting his own back to the bar. He held Sam Beckworth closely against him, and with his left hand drew his gun. He said: "Sam's going over to the jail. Bert, you want to come along, or get out of town? It's your choice."

He waited, apparently sure and easy. Inside, he was in a turmoil of doubt. He didn't know where the bartender stood in this, and the bartender was behind him. He didn't know whether they'd break before him, or destroy him.

Neither did he like the way things had developed. Having made his play, however, he was now prepared to go through with it.

Sam began to struggle, and Coleman increased pressure on the arm. It was touch and go for a moment, and then the tension relaxed. It was Coleman's apparent assurance that did it, his apparent willingness to use his gun if need be. Too, perhaps, Bert and the others were remembering that unhesitating fusillade of bullets that Coleman had poured across the street not long ago.

Bert grumbled: "Hell, it's time I was getting on home anyhow." He turned away, and the others shuffled back to their places at the bar. Coleman walked on out into the night, still holding Sam Beckworth by his twisted and painful arm.

On the walk, he released Sam, saying: "Now go along ahead of me and there'll be no trouble."

Sam spoke over his shoulder, walking: "Friend, enjoy your life while it lasts, because that won't be long."

Coleman grinned without humor. "You've still got your gun, Sam." He shoved his own gun back into its holster. He said: "Turn around and use it if you want."

As soon as he uttered them, he knew the words had been foolish. Just as it was always foolish to prod a man with too much pride. But Beckworth did nothing, and only a slight pause in his stride betrayed his resentment. Coleman knew he now had the little man's bitter and undying hatred.

They reached the jail, and Coleman followed Sam inside. With his right hand he struck a match, holding it high. He said: "Lamp's on the desk, Sam. Light it."

Sam shot him a scowl. Sam had been hoping Coleman would try and light the lamp. He'd apparently been counting on that brief instant when Coleman's eyes would be blinded by the flare. Surlily he lighted a match and held it to the lamp wick. Then he lowered the chimney.

Coleman said: "Keep your back to me. Unbuckle your gun belt and let it drop."

Sam complied, and the gun and belt thudded to the floor.

Coleman murmured, picking up a ring of keys from the desk. "Now go back through that door into the jail. I'll bring the lamp." He followed Sam back to the rear of the building, slammed, and locked the barred door behind him.

Sam went into a cell and sat down on a bench. Coleman set the lamp on a table out of Sam's reach, locked his cell, and went back through the office. He was beginning to feel a sense of aggravation over those wagonloads of wire. Why the devil didn't they get them out of town? Their original pause here had not surprised him. Horses needed resting, and water. But their staying, even after trouble had started over their presence was like a dare, like an open invitation to trouble.

He wished Murphy would return. But it was not yet ten o'clock. Murphy wouldn't be back for another two hours.

He went out into the street again, frowning. Sam Beckworth was in jail, but that did not necessarily mean the trouble was over. The trouble would glow like a bed of coals until those wagons left.

Coleman's jaws clenched with decision. Anger began to stir in him because of this position into which he had been thrust. He was beginning to have a hunch that the wagons had been parked in Troncosa for a purpose, that being to bring the battle into the open.

Perhaps that was not strictly true, for they had been left with only a light guard. And yet . . . ? He had to admit the possibility that the syndicates had set the wagons out as bait, hoping the squatters would take them by force and thus free the syndicates from the restraint of the law.

Walking in the middle of the street, he approached the wagons. The moon was down now, but the stars were bright.

He could see a group of men near the last wagon, and he guessed there must be a dozen of them. If he felt uncertainty, self-doubt, it didn't show. He called: "Who's in charge here?"

There was a murmur from the group.

Coleman said, stopping ten feet from them: "Well?"

A man detached himself from the group and approached Coleman. He was a slight man, his features indistinguishable in the faint light. But Coleman could see the way he walked, could see the low-hung gun that nestled tightly against his thigh.

"I guess I am, friend. What's on your mind?"

"What's your name?" Coleman was blunt, purposely so.

His bluntness had the desired effect. When the man spoke again, his tone showed anger. "Dan Shriver. And you?"

"Coleman." Coleman had heard of Shriver. When you spoke of the Southwest's greatest gunmen, you almost invariably included Shriver's name. The syndicates were hiring talent, no doubt about that. He asked: "Where were you a while ago? Where were you when Sam and Bert took a notion to grab your wagons?"

Shriver's hesitation told Coleman what he wanted to know. He said: "Never mind. I know where you were. You were between here and the river, waiting, weren't you? They'd have stepped into a nice ambush if they'd made it stick, wouldn't they?"

"Smart, ain't you?"

Coleman shrugged. He said: "Harness up and get the devil out of here. I'll give you ten minutes. Get your damned wire out of town!"

"And if we don't?" There was smiling insolence in Shriver's tone.

"I'll take your answer right now. If it's no, we'll save time if you just go after your gun and have it over with."

Never in his life had Coleman made a challenge quite so plain. And he didn't care. Surprisingly he didn't care. He was one man, between two warring factions. He had taken on the job of preserving the peace. Perhaps it was a little unfair that he had

176

been thrust so suddenly into it, with no support from Murphy. But that didn't alter the facts.

The ambush, just thinking of that, angered him. The cold-bloodedness of it appalled him. He was ready in the bright starlight, watching Shriver. He wished he could see Shriver's face, his expression, his eyes. Shriver was undoubtedly wishing the same thing. Coleman opened his mouth to speak again, but stopped himself. You pushed a man so far and no further. Shriver's hesitation, his waiting this long, told Coleman he didn't want a shoot-out now any more than Coleman did.

The tenseness of waiting became intolerable. Every muscle, every nerve in Coleman's body was drawn taut and fine. His left hand was like a claw, waiting.

In the crowd beside the wagons, a man murmured shrilly: "Judas!"

That broke the spell. Shriver's hands dropped easily to his sides. His whole body relaxed, but Coleman's did not—not yet. Shriver said: "All right. We'll go. But we need more than ten minutes. Give us half an hour."

That was Shriver's grasp at pride, his refusal to knuckle under completely. Coleman nodded. "All right. Half an hour." He turned his back and walked toward the Llano.

He was tired, desperately tired. A piano tinkled endlessly. Now a woman's voice began to sing with the piano softly, hauntingly. A couple of dogs began to bark somewhere in town, and it was taken up until there must have been twenty of them barking.

There had been something puzzling about his encounter with Shriver. He had to admit it had surprised him when Shriver had backed down. Before nearly a dozen men, Dan Shriver had refused to draw. Coleman was sure it hadn't been either fear or cowardice that caused his refusal. Then it was either expediency or . . . ?

Coleman fingered the nickel-plated star. Perhaps it was the star that had been the elusive but deciding factor a few minutes ago. Coleman wondered.

He hunkered down against a building face and shaped a cigarette. He lighted it and drew the smoke deeply into his lungs. He could hear the jangle of harness downstreet, the soft curses of the men as they tried to hitch up in the inadequate light. Still he waited, and after a while longer the wagons began to move.

Coleman felt a deep contentment flowing over him. Tonight's task was finished. The wire was on the move, and there would be no opposition to its movement.

Sound of the wagons faded into distance. He could hear faintly a rumble as they crossed the Canadian River bridge. Then all sound was gone, save for the street noises, the shouts and laughter that came from the saloons.

A horse ran along the street and drew up at the sheriff's office. Coleman got up and sauntered that way. Len Murphy swung down, tied his horse. He asked: "Quiet night?"

Coleman grinned. "Not exactly. I was wishing you were here. Bert Flynn and Sam Beckworth tried to jump the wagons. Shriver had a trap laid but it didn't spring. I've got Sam in jail. Thought I'd let him go now."

He went into the jail and unlocked Sam's cell door. "Go on home, Sam. Next time you try to jump the syndicates, do a little checking first. Those wagons were bait for a trap. If you'd got them, you'd have run into as cute an ambush as you ever saw before you got to the river."

Sam was surly, silent. He shambled off toward where his horse was tied before the Llano. He mounted and spurred cruelly down the street. Coleman watched, unspeaking.

Murphy grunted: "Sam's the one they're after. He's the cockiest of the lot. Triple X is after him especially."

Coleman said: "Why?"

Murphy was chuckling softly. "His brand's Four Diamond. It fits over Triple X as neat as anything you ever saw. But if they fence him in at D Cross, he'll have his time findin' any Triple X cattle to run his brand over."

Coleman yawned. "Well, tomorrow's another day. Good night." He crossed the street, hesitated between the hotel and the Llano for a last drink. He chose the Llano and moved that way. He was lonely, and he was beginning to realize that there was no cure for that feeling. He'd made no friends in Troncosa before. He'd make none now.

He had his drink, conscious of the furtive stares of those around him. The feeling of loneliness increased in him. Finally, shrugging, he got up and headed for the hotel.

X

"Dangerous Chance"

Coleman awakened at daybreak, but he did not get up. Deliberately he turned over, determinedly closed his eyes. But he could not sleep. He began to think of the previous night. He began to realize how easily the trouble last night could have flared. His own interference had been reckless, foolhardy. Perhaps it was surprise at its very foolhardiness that had held them in check.

He began to see the size of the task he had undertaken. He wondered if Murphy fully realized it. Two men, standing alone against the bitter enmity that existed between squatters and syndicates. Two men, trying to avert the open warfare which both sides apparently were doing their best to bring about.

He could see that the strategy that had worked last night would not work again. Next time, someone would call him. He'd get off a couple or three shots at most, and then they'd overwhelm him.

Frowning, he rolled out of bed, and dressed himself. He checked the guns and then belted them on. Cramming his hat down over his eyes, he went downstairs.

He found Murphy in the restaurant where they

181

had eaten late yesterday afternoon. Coleman was ravenous. The morning air was cool, pleasant as it blew in the open door behind him. Murphy was eating fried ham and eggs.

Coleman grinned and sat down. "That looks good." He gave his order to the Mexican girl, and leaned back in his chair to wait.

Murphy was watching him oddly. The sheriff wiped his mouth with the back of his hand and said: "Do you know how close you came to being a one-day sheriff's deputy?"

Coleman nodded ruefully. "I thought about it, lying in bed this morning. Brass worked last night, but the same sort of play won't work again."

Murphy frowned. "There's going to be one devil of a fight in this country pretty soon and there ain't a way in the world we can stop it."

"Maybe the syndicates will listen to reason. Who hired that Dan Shriver?"

"Triple X."

"He was behind the ambush plan last night. You reckon it was his own idea, or do you think he was told to do it?"

"His own idea, probably. I don't think Henshaw would go for that kind of tactics."

"Who's Henshaw?"

"Englishman. Manager of Triple X."

"Think he'll listen if we try to talk some sense into him?"

"Might."

"How about riding out there with me this morning? We can see Henshaw, and then stop and talk to Sam Beckworth." Coleman grinned at the sheriff. "I'd like this job to last long enough to collect my first month's pay, anyway."

The waitress brought his breakfast. He attacked it with enthusiasm. Murphy sat picking his teeth, waiting. When Coleman was finished, they went outside and walked the three blocks to the livery barn. Mounted, they moved back through town again, heading for the bridge at the foot of the street.

Shopkeepers were coming from their homes, walking along the streets to work. Children skipped and played on their way to school. The school bell began to ring, a peaceful sound in the clear air. It seemed impossible this morning that violence and bloodshed could have been so near last night.

Coleman realized suddenly that he was enjoying this. This job gave him a purpose, a direction for his life, something he had never had before. He had a job in which selfish concern was secondary, a job that gave him a chance at being important in the lives of those around him.

Admittedly it was more dangerous than a casual riding job. Yet it offered him something a riding job could never offer—a chance to be accepted as a man in the community and not as merely another gunman.

Coleman's horse balked at the Canadian River bridge, but Murphy's animal, being used to it, went out onto the hollow-sounding footing without hesitation. Coleman fought his animal with quirt and spur until the horse, thoroughly frightened, at last burst onto the bridge in panic. His own resounding hoof beats terrified him and he ran in complete terror to the end of the bridge. Coleman was cursing softly, but he could feel no real anger at the horse.

They took a double-track road forking off from the main road here, heading southeast. Murphy kept glancing at Coleman, and once Coleman caught that glance, surprising speculation in it, puzzlement, and something that looked like respect.

Two hours brought them to the scattered, sprawling buildings that marked the headquarters at Triple X. In the center of this jumble of buildings was the ranch house, a towering, three-storied affair whose elegance seemed strangely out of place on the short grass. A few men moved about the yard, working at various tasks, and these stopped to stare at the sheriff and his deputy.

Coleman tied his horse to an iron hitching post whose tip was a lion's head with a ring in its mouth. Their boots made a hollow sound on the porch. Murphy pounded on the door, and after a few moments a woman answered it.

She was a young woman, perhaps twenty-five.

Her hair was piled fashionably high on her head. Her gown was of silk, richly brocaded. Awe came over Coleman at once, and he felt awkward and clumsy. He had never seen a woman like this. Her expression was haughty, but her gray eyes showed noticeable interest in Coleman. "Yes?"

"Your pa home, Miss Constance? We'd like to talk to him a bit." Murphy shifted his tobacco plug from one cheek to the other when he spoke, not awed, unimpressed by the woman's beauty and poise.

She stepped aside from the door. "Come in, please. I'll call him."

Murphy stepped into the house, and Coleman followed. Beneath their feet was the soft-piled depth of Oriental carpeting, a rich, wine-red in color and intricately figured. It was like stepping off the short grass and into some ancient, baronial manor. The furniture was of massive oak, richly carved, beautifully upholstered. Delicate porcelain pieces made splashes of color here and there. Against the walls, paintings hung, oil paintings, and, while Coleman knew nothing of art, he was impressed.

This, then, was the way a cattle king lived. Coleman smiled, comparing this with what Sloan had up in Wyoming. Sloan could probably match Triple X, acre for acre, cow for cow, yet he lived as he'd always lived in a house that was little more than a shack.

He sat down, and after a while he heard steps on the long, curving staircase. Looking up, he saw a tall, lean man coming down. The man's hair was gray, thinning and receding at the temples. He was attired in a tweed coat and riding breeches and boots. Coleman stood up. Basil Henshaw smiled at Murphy and extended his hand to Coleman. Coleman found it thin, but firm and strong. The man spoke with an odd accent, one, Coleman supposed, that characterized all Britons.

Close like this, Coleman had opportunity to study him. The eyes, gray as his daughter's, were keen and intelligent. His friendliness could not entirely erase his hauteur, although it was apparent that he made a sincere attempt to conceal that quality in himself.

"What brings you here, old chap?" he asked the sheriff.

"Trouble." Murphy grinned easily. "There was some wagonloads of Glidden wire come through town last night. I reckon but for Coleman, here, there'd have been some dead men over that wire this morning."

Concern touched Henshaw immediately. "What happened?"

"Why, your man Dan Shriver laid a trap, usin' the wagons as bait. What I want to know is . . . was that trap your idea, or Shriver's?"

"It certainly wasn't mine!"

"Didn't think so. I told Coleman I didn't figure

186

you'd try anything as raw as that." Murphy shifted his chew again. He said thoughtfully: "There's a plenty of trouble over this fencin' without making it any worse. I reckon you know what would happen if two or three or them squatters get killed?"

"The rest of them would probably behave."

"Uhn-uh. You don't know 'em like I do. It'd touch off a range war that wouldn't stop until every mile of fence in the country was torn up by the roots."

"But, man, I've got a right to fence my land. I don't intend to stop."

Murphy grinned wryly. "Ain't much concerned with right an' wrong. I'm tryin' to keep the peace. Shriver's a pushin' man that likes killin'. You keep him here at the ranch unless you want him in jail."

Coleman looked up to see Henshaw's daughter standing in the dining room doorway, watching him. He flushed lightly. Her gaze was intent, and, as she caught his glance upon her, she smiled. There was invitation in her smile, yet it did not entirely erase her hauteur, and the combination of the two things had the effect of angering Coleman. Abruptly he got up and went to the door. On the porch outside he stopped and began to shape a cigarette. The heavy rustling of her dress and the light aura of her perfume made him turn. She had followed him out.

She said: "You're a stranger to the country, aren't you, Mister Coleman?"

He nodded shortly. "You might say that. I've been here a couple of weeks." The girl disturbed him. Her arrogance and her air of superiority angered him. The plain invitation in her eyes, while he could not help being attracted, also angered him.

She laid a light hand on his arm, smiling. "I thought you were. I am sure I would have noticed you had I seen you before."

"Why?" Coleman was blunt. He curbed his desire to walk away from her, to be openly rude.

"Why, you're a very noticeable man. Your white hair sets you apart." She was serene, sure of her attraction. She was a cat, preening on a fence, a mare, biting and kicking at a stallion. It was not her words that gave this impression. It was the heaviness in her eyes, her manner. She was woman, making herself attractive to man.

So sure, so very sure of herself. The kind that likes to play dangerous games with dangerous men. Coleman wondered, suddenly and inexplicably, if she acted with Shriver as she was acting with him.

He had his answer to that almost immediately. Dan Shriver came out of the bunkhouse and approached across the yard. Constance Henshaw's arm dropped immediately from Coleman's and she took a step away from him.

Shriver was white-faced, tight-lipped. His eyes were cold and deadly. Coleman felt a prickle run along his spine. He shot a glance at Constance.

Her eyes were wide, excited, her lips slightly parted, showing a row of firm, white teeth beneath. Her full breasts rose and fell with her quickened breathing. She was watching Shriver with a kind of fascination. Shriver was a slight man, but you could tell, looking at him, that he was tough as whang leather. Slightly bowlegged from riding, his face was sharp, his chin strong and pointed. He wore his hair long, and it was carefully combed and brushed, light in color like desert grass in mid-summer.

A vain man, thought Coleman. A man vain of his attraction for women. A man who was more, Coleman knew instantly, than foreman of Triple X. Shriver was Constance Henshaw's lover.

Yet the danger did not lie in that fact alone. It lay in the difference in their temperaments. Shriver was desperately, insanely in love with Constance. Possessive and jealous, he resented even the touch of her hand on another's arm. Coleman hoped he had not seen the heavy-lidded invitation in her eyes, the slack way her lips pursed.

Constance, on the other hand, was only playing with Shriver. Of that, Coleman was sure. She found him absorbing and interesting at the moment. Tomorrow, it might be someone else. Coleman wondered if she knew what she was trifling with—savage and sudden death for someone. Probably she didn't know.

Shriver stopped at the foot of the steps and stood,

spraddle-legged, watching Coleman coldly. He did not appear to be aware of Constance's presence. He said: "You're a pushin' man, Coleman. You keep it up and you'll push yourself right to the gates of purgatory."

Coleman was momentarily at a loss for words. The light anger that Constance had stirred in him was fanned now by the unfairness of the position into which he had been thrust. He could feel that anger rising in him, dangerously, recklessly. A challenge here, over no more than this would be silly, and Coleman knew it. Yet most challenges sprung from less.

His fists clenched involuntarily at his sides. He said: "Shriver, is last night sticking in your craw, or is it something else?"

He might have expected Shriver to skirt around, but he was disappointed. Shriver said harshly: "Stay away from her."

"From whom?"

Shriver seemed to drop into a half crouch. His voice was almost a snarl. "Don't get smart with me, man. Stay away from Constance."

Without looking at her, Coleman could feel Constance stiffen. Her voice came, sharp and cold: "Now just a minute, Mister Shriver. Just a minute. Aren't you presuming too . . . ?"

"Shut up!" He came up the steps toward her. Her eyes startled Coleman. They were wide and cold, yet filled with wildness that was beyond control.

He passed Coleman and stepped toward Constance. He reached a hand for her.

Fear was in her eyes, yet combined with it was an animalistic anticipation. She feared Shriver, feared his unpredictable temper, his savage disregard for human life. In some way these qualities appealed to the primitive in her, stirred her desire. Coleman could see both the desire and the fear in her eyes. And then her eyes slid away from Shriver's and touched Coleman's own. She was appealing to him for something.

Later, he was to regret what he did then. He answered the appeal in her eyes. His hand shot out and closed over Shriver's right arm. While the man fought for the grip of his gun, Coleman's right came up in a chopping blow to Shriver's throat.

Shriver fell away, choking, gasping for breath. His eyes clung to Coleman, filled with a hatred whose virulence was terrifying. He sat down in the middle of the porch, sucking air into his lungs with a pain-wracked, horrible whistle.

Some inner voice told Coleman: *Kill him now! You're a fool if you don't.*

There was something in Constance's expression repulsive to Coleman. She watched Shriver's struggle for breath, watched his struggle with himself. Shriver wanted to go for his gun. His whole being demanded it. He fought with himself to prevent that until he was fit, until he would have a chance.

Then she turned to Coleman, and it was odd that her voice expressed cultured courtesy while her brain and her soul were so twisted with primitive animal joy. "Mister Coleman, I'm sorry that this happened. Please go before there is more trouble."

He nodded shortly, and stepped down off the porch. He untied his horse and mounted.

This was one of the stupid things that sometimes happened to a man. He felt no desire for Constance. Indeed, if he felt anything, it was repugnance. She had promoted the fight between them to satisfy some ancient, animal longing within herself. Coleman wanted no quarrel with Shriver. Yet now he had one. Shriver would hunt him down, would force a duel with his guns. Shriver would feel the compulsion to expiate what he considered to be an affront to his pride. Since he could not satisfy himself with Constance, whose fault it had been, he would do so with Coleman. It was as simple as that.

Coleman rode out of the yard. Three hundred yards from the house, he reined around to wait for Murphy. He could see the sheriff and Henshaw, on the porch now. Shriver had got to his feet, but he was bent forward a little, as though it still hurt him to breathe. Constance was not in sight, having probably gone back into the house.

Murphy untied his horse, mounted, and rode toward Coleman. His face was grave. "How the devil did that happen?"

Coleman told him.

Murphy scowled. "Damn a woman like that," was all he said, but, when they were almost to town, he added one more thing. "You understand that now Shriver will try to gun you down?"

Coleman nodded. His expression was troubled. Sloan would be coming along one of these days. He had Shriver to think about as well. He was not afraid. Death comes to a man but once. Yet he could not help wondering what quality it was within himself that attracted so much violence and death. And he could not help wondering if he would ever find an end to it. . . .

XI

"Trouble-Making Woman"

Coleman and the sheriff did not go into town. Instead of turning onto the bridge across the Canadian, they kept on along its bank, heading westerly. After several miles of this they came to a fence line. Coleman dropped the gate and led his horse through. Murphy rode after him. Coleman put up the gate again and mounted.

Now Murphy angled away from the river, southward. As he rode, he talked, gesturing with his hands to indicate directions, boundaries, and fence lines. "This here is D Cross. Sam Beckworth's place lies about five miles over thataway in a little draw. Sam's got good water. Mebbe that's the main reason D Cross wants him out."

"Sam own his place?"

"Naw. Nobody owns anything, seems like. D Cross don't own a square inch of land. They lease it. The big outfits ain't bothered squatters like Sam up to now. There was plenty of grass for everybody. But as soon as the fence is finished, it'll be different."

"Why don't Sam and the other squatters do a little leasing themselves?"

"Don't think they haven't thought of it. But you got to know the numbers of the land you want to lease to begin with. Then, if D Cross or somebody else ain't already got it leased, you got to fill out a lot of legal applications for the lease. Chances are, whoever has charge of passin' on the applications is friendly with one or more of the big outfits. So he tips them off when some squatter is tryin' to lease their range. They file an application of their own, an' some way or another, when it turns up, the date on it is earlier than the date of the squatter's application."

"So the squatters get gypped." Coleman was sober.

Murphy grinned at him. "Don't go feelin' sympathetic with the squatters. They been living off the syndicate's beef for years. Take Sam Beckworth for instance. Sam ain't got over a couple of dozen cows in all. But you can make a circle any day of the week around his place an' find upwards of a hundred yearlin's carryin' his Four Diamond brand. Sam's cows are prolific, you might say. Like rabbits. They multiply. But I got an idee that, when the fence is finished between D Cross an' Triple X, Sam's calf crop is goin' to drop off some."

The remaining morning hours passed. Noon came and fell away. In early afternoon, they topped a low rise, and Murphy pulled his horse up shortly. A quarter mile away, nestling in a grove of cottonwoods, was Sam Beckworth's small spread, consisting of a one-room shack and a ramshackle barn built, apparently, out of scrap lumber.

Murphy flung himself from his horse. Coleman saw the blossom of powder smoke down there in the yard. A bullet kicked up dust beside his horse and ricocheted away wickedly. Coleman slipped out of the saddle just as the report reached him. Murphy grunted, his head close to the ground. "Damned fool! Shoot first an' ask his questions later." He raised his head and yelled: "Sam! Hang it, this is Murphy!"

"All right. Come on in." Sam's voice was faint in the still air, but its surly quality was plain.

Coleman grinned at the sheriff. "You reckon it's safe to stand up now?"

"Yeah, I think so." He stood up, a little uncertainly, and waved toward Sam in the yard. Coleman got to his feet, walked a few steps to where his horse stood, and mounted. Together, they rode down the slope into Sam Beckworth's yard.

Sam was scowling fiercely, standing spraddle-legged, defiant, his rifle cradled in his arms. He was like a banty rooster on the prod. "What the devil do you want?"

Murphy was calm, unruffled. "You shoot at all your visitors lately?"

"Since last night I do."

"What happened last night?"

Sam scowled blackly. The scowl made him an almost ridiculous figure. He reminded Coleman of a child, playing at being a man. But Coleman did not make the mistake of underestimating Sam. A man like Sam could be twice as dangerous as a man who was sure of himself.

Sam was silent, as though letting his thoughts ferment into even greater anger than he already felt. Finally he said: "We had a visit from Shriver and some of his Triple X crew. We got invited to pack up and leave inside of twenty-four hours."

"You leavin'?"

"Hell, no! And the first Triple X rider that pokes his nose around here is goin' to get his head blowed off."

Murphy sighed and shrugged helplessly.

Coleman pushed into the conversation: "Sam, supposing nobody bothers you. Will you stay put?"

"Hell, I ain't leaving here. Not till that twenty-four hours is up."

Coleman smiled. "That's good enough. No hard feelings about last night, is there, Sam? You believe that Shriver was gunning for you now?"

Sam was still surly, but there seemed to be no real anger in him. He grunted: "Maybe. I don't know."

Coleman nodded at Murphy, and the two rode away. Both were silent and thoughtful. Murphy frowned at the apparent impossibility of preserving the peace. Finally Coleman said: "If Sam'll stay put, then all we got to worry about is Shriver."

Murphy laughed bitterly. "All? My Lord, man, Shriver's enough."

"Supposing something was to happen to Shriver?"

Murphy shrugged. "I doubt if that would help. Shriver's all that's holding Sam and his crowd back. If Shriver was gone. . . ." He left the sentence dangling.

Coleman supplied: "You think that, if Shriver was gone, Sam and the rest of the squatters would try and put a stop to the fence building?"

Murphy nodded.

Coleman scowled. For a moment, he had considered facing Shriver as he had faced Slick Mercer so long ago. But here the problem was more complex. It was a balance of power situation, and, if Shriver were eliminated, the squatters would become at once the more powerful of the two factions. They, in turn, would abuse their power just as now Shriver and his syndicate cowboys were abusing it.

Determinedly Coleman made his mind wrestle with the problem all the way to town. He had hoped to accomplish something by going out to see the heads of the two factions today. He had to admit that he had accomplished less than nothing. Quite possibly, he had done more harm than good. He had made an implacable enemy of Shrivcr.

Yet he had to concede that even Shriver's enmity

might further the cause of peace. If Shriver's mind were kept occupied with hatred for Coleman, it would have less opportunity to dwell upon his plans for the squatters.

Coleman grinned wryly at the sheriff as he dismounted before the hotel. He asked quietly: "Just what the devil is the use, Murphy? No matter how you look at it, it's an uneasy day-to-day peace. Sooner or later, it's going to bust. Why try to hold it off?"

Murphy didn't return his grin. He said: "Because I took my oath to uphold the law, just as you did. Because a man keeps his word and tries to do his level best."

It was the first time Coleman had seen this deadly seriousness in the sheriff. It was also perhaps the first time he had fully comprehended the meaning of a peace officer's oath. He felt sobered and rebuked. He said: "I wonder if this country appreciates the man they've got for sheriff. I wonder if they do." And he turned away.

He climbed the hotel stairs slowly and thoughtfully. The door of his room was ajar, and he pushed it open.

Constance Henshaw sat in the single chair. She smiled at him as he came in. There was no hesitancy in her smile, nor was there apology. Instead, it came very near being provocative. Again, as she had this morning, Constance angered him. He said harshly: "What are you doing here?"

"I wanted to see you." She stood up. Coleman slammed the door behind him.

"Why?"

"To apologize for the trouble out at the ranch this morning. To ask you to be careful. Dan Shriver is a dangerous man."

"I know that. I didn't need you to come tell me. Does Shriver know you're here?"

Her mouth tightened. "Of course, he doesn't! Do you think I'm a fool?"

Coleman grinned. "Frankly, yes. Nobody but a fool would trifle with Dan Shriver. Now, if you don't mind, I'd like to wash up for dinner. I haven't eaten since early this morning."

Anger blazed openly from her eyes. Her mouth twisted. Coleman could not help comparing her with Ruby, and Constance Henshaw suffered considerably by the comparison. Perhaps this showed in Coleman's eyes.

Constance opened her mouth to speak. Her eyes were blazing, raging, furious. But she did not speak. Before she had the chance, a heavy knocking sounded on the thin door panel. Coleman started. He stared at Constance. His first thought was—*Shriver!*—and he had a sick, hollow feeling in his stomach.

He stepped over to the door, motioning Constance to slip behind it as he opened it. He loosened his guns in their holsters.

He stood utterly still then for a moment, steeling

himself for what he would face when he opened the door. The knocking sounded again and Coleman flung open the door.

Although he had steeled himself for Shriver, it came as a shock actually to see the man there. Shriver was perhaps two inches shorter than Coleman. His eyes were bloodshot, suspicious. He had been drinking—not enough to slow him down, but enough to make him mean, reckless.

"I want to talk to you," he growled.

Coleman stepped toward him, started to pull the door shut behind him. "All right."

Shriver said: "Uhn-uh. Inside."

He crowded toward Coleman, colliding with him as Coleman stood his ground. He stepped back then, leering angrily. "What's the matter, someone in there with you? Some reason why you don't want me in there? You ain't entertaining a woman, are you?"

The nerves in Coleman's body tightened, became fine-drawn, tense. His face was smooth, expressionless. But his eyes were hard. If he let Shriver in that room, nothing on earth could prevent a shooting, or could prevent the death of one or both of them. As it was, Shriver might suspect Constance's presence, but he wouldn't fight because of his suspicions. Not now, anyway. Not just now.

Yet to make an issue of the thing would only confirm Shriver's suspicions. In his mind Coleman cursed Constance Henshaw bitterly. *Damn a trouble-making woman!*

His mind dodged about frantically. Dan Shriver watched him, eyes narrowed, hands ready, even anxious. Coleman knew he'd have to face Shriver before long. But not now. Oh, Lord, not now! Not this way, over a woman that wasn't even worth arguing over. Yet how could he stop it? How in daylight was he going to stop it?

XII

"Mission of Death"

Shriver asked again, narrow-eyed, quarrelsome: "You got a woman in there?"

Coleman closed the door firmly behind him. He said: "Maybe. Maybe not. You can make up your own mind about that. One way or the other, it's none of your blamed business. Do I make myself plain enough?"

Now, he thought, as he watched Shriver's eyes widen. For an instant the two stood in the narrow, dim hallway facing each other. Then, at last, Shriver relaxed. It was quite plain that he thought the woman in Coleman's room was Constance Henshaw. Yet he was not absolutely sure.

Perhaps he saw the signs in Coleman, the signs that told him a fight would be just as inevitable if he forced his way in and turned out to be wrong as it would be if he were right. Abruptly he turned and made steps sounding on the stairs.

Coleman released a long sigh of pent-up breath. And he began to get angry. He waited until Shriver's steps stopped sounding on the stairs, and then he went back into the room. He said harshly: "Get out of here. Get out and stay out. There's enough trouble in this country without you adding to it. You're enjoying the thought of two men fighting over you, but would you enjoy having a man killed over you?"

There was a smile on her face, but her eyes were filled with hate. Somewhere Coleman had bungled his handling of her. Now she would not rest until she had brought about the very thing he sought to prevent. She said softly, nastily: "Afraid?"

He shrugged. "I don't want to kill him."

She began to laugh, low at first, but as her laughter continued, it raised in pitch until it was almost hysterical. Coleman opened the door and pushed her into the hall.

By the time Ruby had been in Mobeetie an hour, she knew she had made a mistake. She had inquired assiduously all over town, but none she asked had seen Coleman.

Then the man she had talked to in Albuquerque had been all wrong. He had guessed it must have been Mobeetie where he had seen Coleman, but apparently he had guessed poorly.

Ruby sat down in the lobby of the hotel, feeling helpless, feeling lost. Tears welled up in her eyes. The search had been too long. Perhaps Coleman had only stopped at Mobeetie for a day. Perhaps that was why no one remembered him. Perhaps he had moved on, south across the limitless, endless plains of Texas.

Ruby was forced to consider the possibility that

she would never find him. He could travel so much faster than she.

Never in all her life had things appeared quite so hopeless. She had less than ten dollars left. Ten dollars didn't carry you very far. So it meant dropping the search for Coleman, going back to work. It meant more waiting, months of it, while she built up another hoard for traveling expenses. By the time she had enough, Coleman's trail would be cold.

She dropped her face into her hands. Despite her control, developed over the past months, her shoulders began to shake with sobs. Desperately she fought to regain control of her slipping emotions. And slowly she regained it. Her sobs slackened. She dabbed at her eyes with her handkerchief, and looked up.

A woman was coming across the lobby. A young woman. A beautiful woman. But the woman's dress was garish, bold. Her face was rouged and hard. Ruby stared at her, dropped her glance as the woman's eyes brushed her.

This time, she had been close—so terribly close. If she'd had just a little more money, she might have. . . . A woman's earning power was pitifully small, waiting on tables, sewing, cleaning. But if a woman were determined enough, if she were willing to earn it as that woman did. . . .

Just the thought of it made Ruby flush deep scarlet. Her mind automatically rejected the idea.

Then she thought of Coleman. She considered the danger, the uncertainty of life to a man who lived by his guns. Delay now might mean that, when she did find Coleman, she would find only a grave.

The blood drained out of her face. Resolutely she got up, and swiftly crossed the lobby.

She caught the woman's arm at the foot of the stairs. "Excuse me, I. . . . Could I talk to you for a moment?"

The woman's glance was hard, suspicious. She stared at Ruby, unmoving, for a long, long moment. Ruby's eyes were pleading, panicked. Finally the woman shrugged. "All right. Come on up. Which one of the rats is yours?"

She started up the stairs, with Ruby a step behind. Irritably she asked, again: "Well, which one do you want me to send packing?"

"I . . . I don't understand."

The woman sighed. They reached the top of the stairs, and she led Ruby into a small, beautifully furnished room. The woman flung her hat onto the bed and sank down beside it. She gestured with a hand at a nearby chair. Ruby sat down uncertainly.

Fear was beginning to eat into her. She wondered if this were where the woman entertained her men. Her hands were trembling, her face pale.

When the woman spoke again, her voice was softer, gentler. "Honcy, my name is Lily. Now what's your husband's name?"

Ruby's voice was a whisper. She was completely confused. "What's that got to do with it?"

"Ain't that what you wanted to see me about? Say, what is this, anyway?"

"I . . . I'm looking for my husband. But I've run out of money. I need a job. I . . . ," Ruby flushed, but she went on determinedly. "A woman like me can't earn very much, but a woman like you. . . ." Ruby stopped, acutely miserable.

"Oh! So that's it? Uhn-uh, honey. Nothing doing."

"I thought, if you'd take me where you work and introduce me. . . ." She couldn't go on. She couldn't say another word.

Lily's voice was bitter. "Men!" she spat. A silence lay over the room for a few moments, and then Lily said resignedly: "Suppose you tell me the whole story."

Ruby cleared her throat and began. She began at the beginning. When she was finished, it seemed she had been talking for hours. Actually it had been less than ten minutes. Lily said huskily: "The guy said it was Mobeetie, huh?"

Ruby nodded.

Lily said: "He ain't been here. Did the guy tell you the name of the saloon where he saw him?"

Ruby frowned, trying to remember.

Lily interjected: "I've worked around most of the towns hereabouts. If he told you the name of the saloon, maybe I could tell you where it was."

"He didn't say." Suddenly Ruby brightened. "He did say something about it, though. He said they kept a cage of rattlesnakes at one side of the door and a cage of Gila monsters at the other, whatever they are."

Lily released a long sigh. "Troncosa, honey. That's the Llano saloon in Troncosa."

Ruby sat very still, not daring to hope, but feeling the excitement surging up within her. "How far is it from here?"

"An eight-hour trip by stage." Lily stared at her thoughtfully. "I hope this man of yours is worth what you're doing for him. I hope you don't get hurt, honey, and that's a fact."

"I won't! Oh, I won't!" She remembered the ten dollars that remained in her purse. "Do you know . . . how much the fare is to Troncosa?"

"Eight or nine dollars, I guess. Something like that." She got up and crossed the room. She opened the bureau drawer. "You clear broke, honey?"

"No. No, I have that much."

"Sure now?"

"Sure." Ruby smiled at her gratefully. "When does the stage leave for Troncosa?"

"Five o'clock. You're lucky about that, too. There's only two of them a week, but there's one going tonight. You'll get there a little after mid-night."

Ruby stood up. "I can't thank you enough."

"I didn't do anything. I hope you find him. I hope he's good enough for you when you do."

Ruby smiled again. But her heart was crying: *Just let him be all right. Just let me find him and let him be all right!* She went out into the hall. There was an eternity to spend between now and five o'clock. There was another eternity to spend while the stage was traveling between Mobeetie and Troncosa. Then she would find Floyd. Then the long search would be over.

A hundred miles west, at this moment, a group of horsemen traveled steadily east. Sloan rode ten yards in the lead, setting the pace, which was a hard and grueling one. Behind him rode five men, the same five who had ridden south out of Wyoming so many months before. One was missing. He had become embroiled in a shooting in Trinidad and was now serving out a thirty-day jail sentence for disturbing the peace.

Sloan was not unaware of the grumbling and complaining his men had been doing lately. He would catch the tail end of a conversation as he came in to the campfire at night from one of his long walks. They weren't man-hunters. They were cowboys. They didn't like the implacability of the way Sloan hated Coleman. They grew uneasy before this obsession that ruled him. They were beginning to think he was touched.

In them, a sort of sneaking sympathy for

Coleman was developing. It was the instinctive sympathy of ordinary men for an underdog. These men had all known Will Sloan. Only their loyalty to Sloan himself kept them going at all, feeling deeply within themselves that Will had been killed in self-defense.

Sloan was aware of all these factors, these feelings in his men. He resented them bitterly. Yet he knew he could not change them, nor would he try, for that would only widen the rift that was developing and might perhaps bring about a final and decisive break between himself and his men.

He couldn't chance that. Losing his men would mean destruction of all his plans, now when they were so near to fruition. So when he sensed rebellion in his men, he babied them with extreme courtesy that came hard to him. As each day passed, his eyes grew ever colder and more determined.

His ranch in Wyoming was forgotten. In his state of mind it was no longer important. Occasionally he would write, or telegraph for money, but that was the total extent of his communication with home. Nor did he ever think of Frank O'Connell, who he had murdered in a fit of frustrated rage, unless it was to consider that even O'Connell's killing had widened the rift between himself and his men.

Troncosa lay ahead, fifty miles ahead. They would camp tonight within twenty miles of it and would reach it in the early morning tomorrow.

Mobeetie lay another fifty miles beyond, and Sloan planned to reach Mobeetie by nightfall tomorrow.

He smiled grimly as he rode, tall and bulky in his saddle. He rode like a cavalryman, left hand holding the reins, right held, stiff and straight, at his side, swinging slightly with the motion of the horse. He rode like a man on a mission—a mission of death.

At times like this, when the land lay, blank and endless, before him, he would sometimes think of Will. Of Will as a baby in his mother's arms. Of Will as a boy, playing at being a man. Of Will's coming home with his first black eye.

Will had been Sloan's bid for eternity. Now that chance was gone. Because a fast gunslinger had shot him down.

In reality, Sloan's feeling for his son had not been a feeling of real affection. It had been too colored with vanity and pride. Will had never been a person to Sloan, a person to be loved, indulged, disciplined. Will had simply been the means for the Sloan name to continue, for the empire Sloan had created to grow.

He had instilled in the boy his own monstrous pride in the creation of his hands—Z Bar. He had instilled in the boy his own arrogance and unscrupulousness. It did not occur to him that these very qualities had brought about Will's death. He had to have someone to blame for Will's death. He couldn't blame Will and he couldn't blame himself. That left Coleman to blame. That left Coleman to kill. When that was done, he could rest. He could go back to Wyoming and to Z Bar.

At dusk he halted his horse abruptly in a small hollow where a spring seeped forth. "All right. Let's make camp."

As men coming out of a trance, his cowboys halted and swung stiffly from their saddles. It was routine, this camping. One man remounted and drove the off-saddled animals off a hundred yards from camp where he halted to let them roll. He would herd them until midnight, when another would relieve him. He left one horse ground-tied in camp for his relief to use when the time came.

A second man unhooked the panniers from the two pack horses and set about unpacking grub for supper. A third and a fourth walked out onto the prairie to gather buffalo chips for a fire.

The last man gathered handfuls of dry grass, piled them, and touched a match to the pile. When the men came in with their armloads of buffalo chips, he added them judiciously to the fire.

The cook went to the seep and dipped up water for coffee. Sloan himself lay down and stared moodily at the sky, resting his graying head on his saddle. A stink rose from the soaked sheepskin lining, from the soaked saddle blanket drying nearby. But it was a familiar stink, the smell of months of rancid sweat moistened and freshened by today's new sweat—rank and sweet like the smell of death.

The smell of death. Sloan permitted himself to think of Coleman. Of Coleman dead, silently rotting in the ground. His thinking gave him a strange sort of pleasure.

Perhaps a sane man might have wondered at this. He might have questioned himself. He might have thought: *God, am I going nuts?* But to Sloan, there was no question of right and wrong. There was no doubt. He loved to kill, and day after tomorrow he would kill.

If he had known of Ruby's mistake, that Coleman was a mere twenty miles ahead in Troncosa, nothing could have held him here tonight. But he did not know. And so he went through the motions of eating, of bedding down under the bright night stars. Around him he heard the gentle, weary snores of the men. With a final curse for Coleman, he slept.

XIII

"Was He a Coward?"

The squatter, Bert Flynn, rode into Troncosa the afternoon after the scrap over the wire. Coleman had deeply humiliated him in the saloon after that affair. Bert had felt guilty about it all night. He had stood beside Sam Beckworth and let Coleman bluff him out. He had allowed Coleman to take Sam and throw him into jail. And he'd gotten out of town at Coleman's contemptuous demand, like a whipped dog with his tail tucked tightly down between his legs.

All during the ride home, all during his solitary supper and during the hours when he'd tried to go to sleep, he had wondered why. Was he a coward? He'd never thought so. Why, then, had Coleman found it so easy to back him down?

The more he questioned himself, the more puzzled he became. If Coleman had been one of those cruel, callous, hard-eyed gunmen, perhaps Bert could have understood. But Coleman was not that. He was calm and easy and sure. He was a man who could smile. Perhaps he was also a man deadly with his guns. But Bert had faced guns before without quailing.

The question in his mind demanded an answer. He woke to that demand, and it pestered him all morning and part of the afternoon. At last, unable to stand it longer, he saddled up and rode toward town. As he came abreast of the Plains Hotel, Shriver came bursting out through the doors. Shriver was plainly beside himself with rage. Bert prudently dismounted, standing behind his horse's head until Shriver had turned his back to head downstreet toward the Llano.

A moment later, Constance Henshaw came out of the hotel, also quite obviously furious. Bert frowned with puzzlement. Something told him that anything that could make Shriver and Constance rage should please Bert Flynn.

He tied his horse thoughtfully. He wondered if maybe he shouldn't turn around and ride out to Sam Beckworth's place. Sam would want to know about this.

But he shook his head. About what? He knew that Shriver was upset, was murderously angry. He knew that Constance Henshaw was equally angry. But that was all he knew. It might add up to something, and it might not. He had to stay in town. He had to try and find out what was in the wind.

He stood uncertainly beside his horse, wondering how he would obtain the information he needed. Bert Flynn was a little slow-witted. He was frowning with puzzlement as Coleman came out the hotel door.

Coleman stopped when he saw Bert. He seemed on the point of turning toward him. It occurred to

Bert that maybe Coleman was going to order him out of town again. He wondered what he would do if that happened. Pride demanded that he tell Coleman to go to hell.

But he knew he wouldn't do it. There was something compelling about this new sheriff's deputy. Bert was aware suddenly, with an accompanying empty feeling within him, that, if Coleman ordered him out of town, he would go without protest.

Coleman only nodded at him, saying—"Hello, Bert."—and stepped into the street. Bert watched him cross, slowly and deliberately. Constance Henshaw, a hundred yards up the street, stopped and turned to watch, also. Coleman went into the restaurant.

Bert shrugged. Shriver had gone into the Llano. The Llano was the only logical place a man could go for information. Stifling his fear, his doubt, his awareness that a squatter's presence in the Llano might be enough to set Shriver off, he went down the walk and entered the saloon.

Len Murphy finished his dinner. For a while he still sat at the table, picking his teeth contentedly, letting the saddle stiffness seep slowly out of him in this restful position. He was slumped down in the straight-backed chair, feet stretched out before him under the table. His shoulder blades rested against the chair back.

Across the street he saw Shriver come out of

the Plains Hotel, followed shortly after by Constance Henshaw. He saw Bert Flynn, saw Coleman come out of the hotel, speak to him, and come toward the restaurant.

Murphy suddenly had an odd, cold feeling in his stomach. It was a thing he had never felt before. If he had been a man given to mental imagery, he might have likened it to the cold grip of death's icy fist. Being the sort of man he was, he smiled inwardly and dismissed the feeling as justifiable uneasiness.

He knew he was dealing with highly explosive ingredients here in Troncosa. Shriver, dangerous under any circumstances, was doubly so now that he had become so insanely jealous of Coleman. What Shriver would do in the next twenty-four hours was a matter for conjecture. But it was almost certain that he would do something. Something rash perhaps—something cold-bloodedly murderous. Like burning out Sam Beckworth.

Coleman came into the restaurant, saw Murphy, and walked toward him, smiling. Yet in spite of that smile, Murphy could sense in Coleman the same intolerable tension that he felt himself.

Coleman pulled out a chair across from Murphy and sat down. The waitress came and stood at his shoulder, waiting for his order. Murphy glanced across the street, saw Bert Flynn hesitate a moment, and then head for the Llano.

Coleman gave his dinner order to the waitress.

Uneasiness kept growing in Murphy as he thought about Bert Flynn and Shriver together in the Llano. Hang Bert, anyway! He ought to have more sense. With things as they were, he ought to know enough to get out of town and stay out. That was the trouble with men. They didn't always do the sensible thing. Sometimes they let their pride drive them to actions they knew to be foolish, even stupid.

Murphy stood up. "I'm going over to the Llano for a while. See you later."

"Sure." Coleman hesitated a moment, concern showing in his face. "Be careful, Sheriff. Shriver's been eating raw meat today."

Murphy grinned. But his grin was less hearty for the recurrence of that cold feeling in the pit of his stomach. It was almost like a premonition. It was almost like a warning not to go over to the Llano.

Murphy was like other men in one respect. He had his share of pride. He was the law in Troncosa, and, if he let a chill knot in his guts rule him, he'd be finished. He said—"All right. I'll be careful."—and went out.

He paused on the walk to fish a cigar out of his upper vest pocket. Carefully he pared off the end with his pocket knife and put it into his mouth. Deliberately he lighted it. Then, puffing with obvious pleasure, he angled across the street toward the Llano.

Thinking of Coleman, he felt a tremendous gratitude. It was rather odd, the way he thought of

Coleman. He had known the man hardly more than two weeks, yet it almost seemed as though he had known him all his life. Since yesterday, Coleman had become a wall at his back as he faced the town, an assurance that they couldn't surround him, couldn't overwhelm him.

He could admit now the awful, devastating aloneness he had felt before Coleman's acceptance of the deputy's star. One man against the town. One man against the endless miles of bleak range. Now it was two men who faced the country. Two men, and neither of them afraid.

Murphy was not a man to stand and look back along the trail at events long finished and past. For some reason, today was different. At odd times, all day, he had caught himself remembering. Remembering the men who had fallen before his guns. Remembering the very few women who had touched his life with their sweetness.

There had been little of real friendship in his life. Lately, since he had been a law officer, there had been respect, given at first reluctantly, lately more wholeheartedly. Coleman was perhaps the first real friend Murphy had had, and that was almost as odd as the fact that he'd not had friends before. For he had only known Coleman a couple of weeks. How could he consider him a friend already? And yet he did. There was no denying it.

Feeling somehow warmed inside, Murphy stepped into the Llano. Shriver brooded surlily over a glass and bottle at one end of the bar. Bert Flynn, at the other end, seemed to be trying to make himself inconspicuous.

Murphy stepped up to the center of the bar, putting himself between them. Feltzer, looking scared, pushed himself away from the backbar where he had been leaning, and stopped before Murphy with both hands flat on the bar. "Drinking, Sheriff?"

Murphy shook his head. "Just ate. Later, maybe." He felt the need for some explanation of his presence here, and so he said: "Man feels the need for someone to talk to sometimes."

"Sure, I know." Feltzer was an odd-looking man, so bald, so bulbous of eye, but Murphy liked him.

With both of them admitting a need for talk, it was odd then that they did not talk. Down at the end of the bar, Shriver drummed ceaselessly on the polished bar top with his fingers. At the other end, Bert Flynn seemed to shrink, to try desperately to make himself invisible. Why didn't Flynn leave if he felt so blamed uncomfortable? Murphy knew the answer to that one. Pride kept Bert here. The same kind of pride that had made Murphy come in, even though he knew it to be dangerous and foolish.

With a light shrug, Murphy turned from the bar and walked across to the glass case that contained the Gila monsters. Thoughtfully he stared down through the glass at these, the ugliest of all of nature's monstrosities. Dull-black and yellow-mottled, unhealthy-looking, they were deadly poisonous, sluggish, fat, bulbous lizards over a foot long. Murphy had heard it said Gila monsters were not, in reality, lizards. He had heard that no lizard is poisonous, that, therefore, the Gila monster could not be one. Maybe not. But if they weren't lizards, he was hanged if he knew what they were.

The sound behind him was sudden and explosive—Shriver, smashing a whiskey bottle against the edge of the bar. As Murphy turned, he heard Feltzer's exclamation of protest that dwindled into immediate nothing.

He turned, nerve-tight, as Shriver began to talk. Shriver's voice was low, angry, mean. "Damn you, Flynn, you came in here tryin' to start trouble with me! I been tryin' to hold myself in, but I'm through with that. You stinking son-of-a-bitch, you want trouble so damned bad, draw your iron!"

The cold feeling was back in Murphy's stomach, was worse now. Bert Flynn, who had glanced nervously at Shriver when he smashed the bottle, now turned a sickly shade of gray. He stepped out away from the bar. There was the contemplation of death in his eyes, panic, perhaps, but no hesitation. Murphy knew in another instant he would draw. And Shriver would kill him. Shriver would kill him, and for one reason only—to satisfy his own murderous, frustrated anger at Coleman.

Murphy said sharply: "Bert! Don't be a damned fool! Keep your hands away from your gun!"

Bert Flynn's voice was plaintive with righteous anger. "Sheriff, I can't do that. You heard what he called me. I ain't afraid of him."

Murphy had slowed Bert, though. He had made Bert think. He turned his glance to Shriver. Then he began his slow movement toward the bar. He intended to put himself directly between the two, hoping thus to prevent this threatened gun play.

The spark was glowing here. The spark needed to plunge the whole country into open warfare. If Bert were killed, the squatters would go hog-wild. If Shriver were the one killed, and that seemed unlikely, the result would be the same. Shriver was the balance of power. With him gone, the squatters would be almost sure to win the battle they were as certain to start.

Murphy said: "Shriver, if you draw your gun, you'd better get me first. Because I'm going to draw against you."

He moved into the line of fire between the two. He was betting that Bert would stay cool, would hold his fire. It was the one imponderable in this war of nerves.

Fleetingly he thought of Coleman, across the street eating his dinner. Desperately he wished Coleman were here. That fist-sized lump of ice in his entrails kept growing larger. It was almost as though he had already begun to die inside.

And then Murphy knew for sure. Perhaps he had guessed before that today was his day to die. But now he knew it was. Somewhere he would miscalculate, perhaps had already done so. Something was going to go wrong here in a second or two, and Murphy would feel the smashing blow of a .44 slug.

Shriver, his eyes wild with hate, moved a step to one side, apparently to bring Bert Flynn into his vision again.

Maybe Bert misinterpreted his move. Maybe panic got the best of him. At any rate, Murphy heard a scuffle, a rustle of movement behind him as Bert went for his gun.

Murphy was fast. But Shriver was a streak of light. His hand hardly seemed to move yet it blurred with motion. One instant his hand was empty, the next it held a gun. His thumb was curled up over the gun's hammer.

Murphy's gun came up, not much behind Shriver's. Behind Murphy, Bert lost some time stepping away from the bar so that he could shoot without hitting the sheriff. Shriver showed then the kind of gunman he was. He showed that he was as good as the best. Unhesitatingly he appraised Bert's move and made up his mind. His bullet drove into Murphy's chest. The hammer of the sheriff's gun fell, but his shot went wild.

Shriver's second bullet tore into Bert's right shoulder, and spun him around before he could even fire. His gun dropped onto the floor. He reeled against the bar and hung there, bleeding on the polished bar top. His face was gray, his eyes filled with shock.

Shriver would have driven him against the bar with a second shot, but Feltzer shoved a shotgun barrel against his side, reaching across the bar to do it. "No more. No more, I said!"

Murphy was conscious, barely conscious, and he knew it was over. He didn't see Shriver go, but he knew Shriver was gone. Then Feltzer was around on his side of the bar, kneeling beside him. Feltzer said hoarsely: "Len! Len, where did he hit you?"

Murphy grimaced when he tried to grin. "Where he aimed to git me." He heard the slam of the door and the pound of running feet. There was another face looking down at him, a face topped with white hair. Coleman.

There was no use now in arguing. He hadn't the strength for it. Besides, he could see by Coleman's expression that it had been the same with Coleman as it had with him. Friendship was between them, and perhaps a kind of kinship of lost souls. Coleman would go after Shriver. There was no stopping that. It was the thing they had talked about, almost a code. Kill a lawman and you've got another to face.

So Murphy didn't use his last strength for argument. Only for warning. He whispered: "Be careful. He's . . . fast. Awfully fast."

XIV

"Tall and Powerful"

The shots had drawn a small knot of people to the front of the Llano. Fearfully they began to drift in through the doors. There was universal shock in them at seeing Murphy dead. Bert Flynn hung from the bar, desperately holding on until the doctor came in and led him away to Feltzer's office in the rear where there was a leather-covered couch.

Coleman helped Feltzer to lift Murphy's body to one of the tables. Then he strode outside.

The sun lay low now upon the western horizon. At this time of day, it put a sort of orange glow on everything it touched. Coleman's face was somber, saddened. He kept telling himself that, if he had gone with Murphy a while ago, he might have prevented this.

As had Murphy, Coleman had keenly felt the kinship that was growing up between them. Now he felt a terrible sense of loss. He turned toward the hotel where his horse was racked and saw Constance Henshaw standing there. Her face was frightened as though she were realizing for the first time what a dangerous game she had played.

Coleman stopped on the walk, facing her. "Where will he go?"

"To Triple X, I suppose. Where else?" Her voice lacked life and warmth. It was dead, still with shock. But the need she felt for explanation was there in her eyes. She groped for words. "I . . . I didn't know . . . I didn't realize. . . ."

Coleman's tone was gentler than any he had used with her before. No. She hadn't realized. How could she? In England, where she'd been raised, they didn't have men like Shriver. She'd been playing with a man. She hadn't quite believed she was playing with a killer. Coleman said: "Don't blame yourself. This has been coming for some time now." He untied his horse's reins and swung to the saddle.

He rode south to the bridge and out across its hollow-sounding length.

As he had done early this morning, he again took the two-track road that led to the left. The prints of a running horse were plain here, telling him that his quarry had, indeed, headed for Triple X.

He wished he'd taken time to get a fresh mount from the livery barn. This horse was tired, sluggish. There was no real hurry, though. There was plenty of time. Shriver wouldn't run. Coleman occupied himself, as he rode, with thoughts of Murphy, with recollection of all that had happened in the last two days. It was as though he had himself walked into a powder-keg situation, providing the fuse by his presence.

No, he convinced himself in all fairness, *all of it*

was not my doing. Last night I prevented Shriver's trap from springing. Last night, I prevented killing.

Nor had he been responsible for Murphy's death. Perhaps, if blame must be laid somewhere, it should be at Constance Henshaw's door. She was responsible for Shriver's vicious mood today.

Coleman shrugged. What use to lay blame for something that was done? Everyone made their share of mistakes. He doubted if Constance would ever make this particular mistake again.

The sun went down, and the soft, gray-violet of dusk sifted across the land. Coleman rode steadily, taking from his horse all that he thought it safe to take. A mile from Triple X headquarters, he met Basil Henshaw, driving a black buggy at a reckless clip. He raised a hand, and Henshaw drew his horse to a plunging halt.

Coleman asked: "Shriver at the ranch?"

Henshaw nodded. The man was frightened. He said: "This is a beastly business! He's back there, talking to my crew. He says he's killed the sheriff and now's the time to wipe out the squatters. I tried to talk some sense into him. I ordered my men to disregard his orders. I even discharged him!" Henshaw's voice had risen with incredulous disbelief. "He wouldn't discharge, old chap. He . . . he threatened to kill me!"

Coleman said: "All right. Go on into town. Your daughter is there. I'll see what I can do with Shriver." He sat his horse in the middle of the road until the buggy disappeared in its own cloud of dust.

The job of taking Shriver began to look more difficult. Coleman debated for a moment. Should he ride on to Triple X and get a fresh horse? Or should he cut across country now, crowding the remaining strength out of the animal he was riding? He decided on the former, believing not only that it would put him at Sam Beckworth's place sooner, but that there was a bare possibility Shriver and his crew had not yet left.

He kicked his horse into a shaky-kneed trot and fifteen minutes later rode into the yard at Triple X.

A man peered at him from the lamp-lighted door of the cook shack. Coleman called: "Shriver left?"

"Uhn-huh."

"How many men with him?"

"Four. The rest refused to go."

"Where are they?"

"In here."

Coleman dismounted and walked to the door. The cook shack was combined with the bunkhouse, occupying one end of it. Between was a cleared space in which were two long tables. There were half a dozen men sitting at one of the tables, eating.

They looked at Coleman expectantly and he said: "Shriver killed Sheriff Murphy a while ago. I guess you know that. I want him. I want a posse to help me get him."

A young, black-haired youngster at the end of the table looked at him with a mocking grin. "Scared?"

Coleman shook his head. "I want Shriver. I don't give a hang about the men with him. But I can't get Shriver if I have to fight four others first."

A middle-aged, graying man with a bushy mustache, sitting next to the kid, said: "Hey, you really ain't scared, are you?"

"No."

There was a sound of scuffling feet as the men got up, all six of them. The black-haired youngster, sobered, said: "You got your posse, mister."

"I need a fresh horse."

"I'll get him for you."

The six filed out into the night. The cook handed Coleman a cup of coffee, and Coleman stood in the door, sipping it, looking out, and waiting.

There was an edge of impatience in him now. Previously taking Shriver away from a sizeable crew of men had loomed before him as an all but impossible task. He had not shirked it in his mind, yet he had realized its futility. Now he had a chance—a good chance. The very fact that his posse was composed of Triple X riders would reduce the likelihood of violence between him and the riders with Shriver.

He finished his coffee and turned to set the cup down. Then he went outside. The noise at the corral increased as the Triple X posse mounted.

The black-haired youngster led a horse up to Coleman, who took the reins from him.

All of them milled around him now. He said: "You know this country better than I do. If there's a short way to Sam Beckworth's, let's take it."

Almost as one man, they kicked their horses and lined out across the plain at a steady lope.

At the onslaught of darkness, Sam Beckworth began to feel a rising uneasiness. He had eaten supper before dark and had washed up the dishes immediately. As dusk darkened the land, he had lighted no lamp. For a long time he sat, silent and thoughtful, inside his cabin.

Sam was one of the smallest of the squatters. There was only himself here, only himself. Yet he knew he was the one Shriver would go after. For one thing, Sam never took any but Triple X cattle, which made him Shriver's special problem. For another thing, Sam was the accepted leader of the squatters. He was the firebrand, the one who was behind every squabble that started.

He began to think of last night. That blamed new sheriff's deputy! Why hadn't he stayed out of it? Why hadn't he let him and Bert alone?

There was no real doubt in Sam Beckworth's mind as to whom his chief enemy was. That was Shriver and there could be no doubt of it. But this Coleman, this new sheriff's deputy—he offered a threat, too. Not only had he stopped the destruction of the wagons, he had humiliated Sam as well, had thrown him into jail like a quarrelsome drunk.

Shriver was the main problem, the one to be taken care of first. After that, he could think of Coleman.

He grinned at his own thoughts nervously. Here he was worrying about Coleman, thinking about taking care of Shriver, while at this moment Shriver might be on his way here, to kill Sam and burn him out.

Sam was conscious of an overpowering feeling of aloneness. He wished he had someone to talk to, someone to back him up if Shriver did come.

The more he thought of it, the more foolish it seemed for him just to sit here and wait, a sitting duck for Shriver when and if he did come.

Suddenly Sam got up. He dug down under his mattress and got the small leather pouch of gold that was his total worldly wealth. Taking up his rifle, he went outside.

The cabin didn't matter particularly. It wasn't home; it was only a shelter, a place to sleep. Sam's real wealth lay not in the land, or the shack and corrals, but in the cattle, branded Four Diamond, that roamed the plain.

Why, then, should he stay, risk his life in defense of something that had no value to him?

The answer was simple. He shouldn't. Decisively he went to the corral and saddled a horse. There were two more horses there. He turned them out and watched them disappear into the darkness. He mounted, then, and took a course away from Triple X. He rode up on a little knoll, dropped into a hollow, and climbed out onto a higher knoll beyond it. Here he dismounted. He tied his horse to a clump of yucca and settled down on his haunches to wait.

Likely they'd surround his place and ride in from all four sides. That was why he had come this far, to the second rise instead of the first. He wondered what he would do when they did come. Would he watch helplessly, not interfering? Or would the anger take him, would his rage make him belly down and throw bullets into their midst? He didn't know yet. He'd wait and see how things shaped up.

The minutes slipped away, endlessly. Sam began to wonder if Shriver would come. An hour passed, part of another. He was about to give up his vigil when he heard the distant pound of horses' hoofs.

There was no counting them. But it was plain to Sam that there were several. After a moment, the pounding stopped. He laid down and put his ear to the ground.

For a full ten minutes he heard nothing at all. Then he saw the skylighted silhouette of a horseman before him, on the knoll between himself and his cabin. The horse and man disappeared, and after a few moments Sam heard a shout, a few minutes later a volley of shots.

Without conscious thought, Sam sprang to his

feet and ran to his horse. He swung into the saddle and drove the animal down through the hollow and onto the knoll where he had seen the lone horseman.

Below him, from here, he could hear their voices as they searched through the cabin and the rickety barn. He reined up and dismounted. He led the horse back a dozen yards and tied him securely, carefully. Then he went back to the crest of the knoll and bellied down, his rifle before him.

Damn them, they weren't going to get off scot-free! Sam seemed almost calm. He waited. After a few moments, he saw a flicker of flame inside the cabin. Anger raged through him. The fire inside the cabin grew rapidly. Another fire blossomed inside the barn. He saw the five clustered in the yard, watching, waiting until the flames would be beyond a man's ability to control or halt.

The light in the yard grew. Sam sighted carefully along his rifle barrel. One shot—maybe two. That's all he'd have if he wanted to live. He picked a man that was about Shriver's stature. You couldn't tell, at this distance, in this light. You had to guess. Sam hoped he would guess correctly.

The man's back came over his sights. He centered, steadied, held his breath as he squeezed down on the trigger. The rifle bucked against him.

It was a temptation to waste a moment here, to wait and watch the man he had hit go down. But Sam didn't do it. Before the group below him could spring into movement, he centered on another man and squeezed down again.

They were scrambling for cover now, ludicrously startled, frightened. Sam took an instant to stare down into the yard.

One man lay utterly still, crumpled, broken. Another man was down, but stirring. Sam heard Shriver's ragged, furious shout: "Get mounted! It's Sam! Get after him!"

Sam turned and ran. His fingers were all thumbs as he untied his horse. He mounted, awkward with haste, and drove his spurs viciously into the horse's sides. As he rode, he shoved the rifle down into the saddle boot. He was cursing softly, but he was not displeased. He hated to have missed Shriver. But he had taken a toll for the loss of his cabin and barn. Maybe later tonight, he could take a fiercer toll.

He headed his horse toward town, demanding with his raking spurs every bit of the horse's speed. An odd exhilaration possessed him. This was the first time Sam had taken a human life. He felt no remorse, no guilt at all. He had proved something to himself. He had proved that a small man can be just as deadly as a big one. He had proved, against overwhelming odds, that a small man, not bothered by scruples and inhibitions, is the equal of several big men.

The knowledge was like alcohol in his blood stream. It was intoxicating. Sam felt tall and powerful. The pound of his horse's hoofs was thunder beneath him, the air a stiff wind in his face. Suddenly the still night air echoed with Sam's shouted laughter. He knew what he would do when he got to town. Released from the controls that society puts upon a man, he could kill Shriver and every one of his men before the night was out. Town was a paradise for the dry-gulcher. And Sam would use the town skillfully tonight.

He began to laugh again.

XV

"$500 Apiece"

Sloan didn't know how long he had slept. Nor did he know what had awakened him. He lay, unmoving, staring up at the stars, listening. It lacked an hour or more of being midnight. The stars told him that. The minutes ticked away. His ears strained for sound. One of his men was snoring lustily. The others were quiet, breathing softly.

Then Sloan heard it. It was a sound composed of many small sounds, the tinkle of a cinch buckle, the slap of saddle against the back of a horse, the fidgeting of a horse's hoofs and its small grunt as the cinch was jerked tight.

Sloan turned and counted the lumpy shapes beyond the smoldering embers of the fire. Three. One was night-herding the horses. That meant one was leaving. Only one.

For a moment, his rage at the desertion controlled him. He came very close to springing up, to shouting the others awake. But then he relaxed. He was as close to his quarry as he had been for months. He would not risk everything to hold one man that wanted to desert.

If the truth were known, Sloan was afraid. He was afraid that the rest of his crew, instead of helping him to halt the deserter, would join him instead.

Let him go, then. Let him go and then wake the others. Offer them $500 apiece, if need be, and go on tonight. Keep them riding until they were so tired they couldn't think. Let them think about money instead of about human mercy for a change. $500 was well over a year's wages. They'd forget desertion and pity for Coleman if he gave them a chance to earn that much in less than two weeks.

He waited, then, until the lone deserter had ridden off into the night. And he waited some more, until there was no possibility that the man remained within earshot. Then he got up, shouting: "All right! Roll out! We're goin' on tonight!"

They came out of their blankets, grumbling. Sloan waited until they were fully awake, watching them with wary eyes. Edgerton was the one who was gone. Sloan had guessed that even as he had watched the man ride away. Edgerton was the one who had brought them toward Mobeetie with his cryptic note. But Edgerton had been the brooding one since then. Edgerton had been the malcontent.

Sloan knew why. Edgerton had met Coleman's wife on the Mobeetie stage. Sloan's lips curled. Edgerton was young. He'd probably fallen for her. He was regretting his betrayal of her.

Sourly the men got up. One of them went after water while another built up the fire. Sloan brought in the night herder with a hoarse bellow. Then he dug a brown bottle from his saddlebags and uncorked it, passing it around.

When each of them had taken two stiff drinks, he smoked. "I want to go on tonight. I don't want to stop again until we find him. But I'll make it worth your while. You've been drawing a bonus ever since we started hunting him. Now I'm going to offer you a real bonus. Five hundred dollars apiece when we get him."

"What if we don't?" The protest was half-hearted, colored with excitement at the prospect of earning that much money.

Sloan, the gambler, threw everything he had into the pot. There came a time when you had to bet the world. This was one of those times. He said: "If we haven't got him in two weeks, you each get your five hundred. You can quit. And I'll go on alone."

He surprised them and took the protest out of their thoughts. There wasn't one of them now that could be driven away. Money had accomplished what loyalty no longer could. "All right," he said, "get your coffee then, and we'll be going."

He walked down to the seep and doused his head with water, rubbing the sleep out of his eyes. Excitement began to work through him. He felt pleased with himself. He had turned what could have been disaster into advantage. The night herder drifted the horses into camp, and each man roped his own.

When Sloan returned to the camp, they were

tying their blankets on behind their saddles. A couple of them were hanging the panniers on the pack animals. The grumbling was gone out of them. They could see the end now, and they could think about what they would do with $500.

Sloan grinned sourly. He knew two of them that would spend the money over a bar. They'd wallow in the gutter until it was gone. Whoever robbed them would be doing them a favor. $500 was too much to try and drink up without stopping.

One of the others, Burwell, would use the $500 to get married on, if the girl was still waiting. That worried Burwell. It had worried him all along. The girl was pleasure-loving. Sloan thought it likely that she was already married to someone else. She wasn't one to sit around home and wait for a man.

The fourth, Jethro, would use the money as a down payment on that ranch he was always talking about.

Sloan took his horse's reins from Jethro, who had caught the animal. He led him over to where his saddle and blankets lay. By the time he had finished saddling, the others were ready, grouped around him. He swung to his saddle.

For a moment, he stared at the sky, getting his bearings by the stars. Then he set out at a steady lope toward Troncosa, which lay in a direct line between where they now were and Mobeetie.

They ought to strike a road before too long. That would speed the rate of their travel.

Sloan found it hard to control his exultation. He

had missed Coleman twice now—by the barest of margins. This time was going to be different. This time Coleman wasn't going to get away. Sloan's eyes took on a bright, glittering look. His mouth was a thin, cruel line.

Once, he might have played this game by the rules. But that time was long ago. He had forgotten the rules somewhere back along the hundreds of miles he had traveled in search of vengeance. He had been cheated of his vengeance, once by a trick, once by a few minutes of time. He would not be cheated again. He would shoot Coleman from in front, from behind, in any circumstances or place in which he might find him. There was only one must in Sloan's mind. It couldn't be too quick. *Gutshoot him*, he cautioned himself, *so that he'll know who did it, so that he'll suffer a while before he dies.*

Sam Beckworth's shack and barn were hot, glowing coals by the time Coleman and his posse reached them. Built of sun-dried scrap lumber, they had probably burned completely in less than half an hour. There was yet a little light from the smoldering rubble, and by this light Coleman dismounted to look at the men on the ground.

One was dead. The second was shot through the lungs and dying fast. But he got out a few words. "Sam . . . was gone when we . . . got here. Shriver fired the buildings. When there was light enough, Sam opened . . . up on us. Got me with the . . .

second shot." The man began to cough. Blood flecked his lips.

Coleman asked: "Where'd Shriver go?"

He didn't think the man was going to answer. But at last the words came, faint and weak. "Town, I guess. He was . . . chasin' Sam."

Coleman was reluctant to leave. He knew he couldn't load this man and take him into town. Nor would the man last until a doctor could be brought to him. So Coleman waited, feigning unconcern and patience until the man drew his last breath. Then Coleman laid him back on the ground.

He covered the two with his own two blankets, untied from behind his saddle. The men with him were grumbling angrily because Shriver had gone off and left a wounded man behind with no one to care for him. It rankled in them. All of them realized that any of them, at any time, might be called upon to give his life in defense of Triple X. But they didn't like this leaving a man as though he were a discarded piece of equipment. Coleman said: "You can come back for them in the morning. Ought to have a wagon, anyway."

He mounted and led out toward town. He knew it would be past midnight before he arrived. That didn't mean anything. Neither Sam nor Shriver, or Coleman would sleep tonight. Tonight was the night for the showdown. Sam would want Shriver, and Shriver, Sam. Coleman wanted Shriver, alive if possible for Murphy's murder. He wanted him dead if it wasn't possible to get him alive. But he didn't want Sam to get Shriver. And he didn't want the thing to flare into a full-scale range war.

It wouldn't, either, if it could be settled tonight, before there was time for the syndicates to gather their cowpunchers in off the range.

Coleman tried to decide what Murphy would want done. Murphy would put keeping the peace ahead of vengeance for his own killing. Coleman could not do that. Vengeance against Shriver came first. Yet, maybe the two things were the same. With Shriver gone, the squatters would have the upper hand. Coleman himself, as the law, could step in and assume Shriver's position as the pro-tector on the side of the syndicates, thus main-taining the balance of power.

He began to feel a little hope. The men at his back could give him little assistance in handling the situation. All they could do would be to keep Shriver's two men off of him. But that would be enough. He thought it would be enough.

In spite of Coleman's optimism, and the men at his back, he felt an odd and incomprehensible uneasiness, as though there were something he had not considered in this game of nerves, as though there were some force he had not reckoned with, some force that could upset all his calculations, wreck all his plans.

As, indeed, there was such a force. Sloan even now was approaching Troncosa at a steady trot.

XVI

"Small and Quick"

Most of the town was dark as Coleman rode across the bridge. There were a few lights. The stage depot, a block from the bridge, was lighted by a single lamp inside on the counter. Coleman could hear the jangle of harness behind the adobe building as hostlers caught and harnessed relief teams for the incoming stage.

At the next corner he halted. The Triple X riders with him also halted, grouped around him. Coleman said: "Let's separate. Circulate around a little. I'll be in front of the Llano in thirty minutes. If you find out anything, let me know then." He was silent, thoughtful, for a moment. At last he said: "You're working for the sheriff's office. Can you remember that? Triple X and its quarrels are none of your business tonight. I want you to avoid trouble. I don't want any of you to shoot unless you have to in order to save your lives. Do you all understand?"

He got a low murmur of assent from the group.

He said: "All right, then, thirty minutes."

He turned off here at the corner and rode alone along the dark and silent street. It was unusual for the saloons to be open tonight, but three of them were open, the Llano being one of them.

An illusion of brooding tenseness seemed to pervade the air of the town. Somewhere was Sam Beckworth, hidden in darkness. Also, somewhere in the town, roaming the streets searching for Sam, was Shriver and his two remaining Triple X riders.

Coleman rode a circle through the town, seeing nothing, hearing nothing. He dismounted two blocks above the Llano, and tied his horse to a nearby rail. Then he continued afoot.

He could see the glow thrown on the street from the lobby lights of the Plains Hotel. Henshaw would be there. Probably Constance Henshaw could be found there as well.

Coleman grinned uneasily. He had never faced anything quite like this before. Sam was lurking somewhere, waiting for a shot at Shriver. Shriver and his two prowled the dark streets looking for Sam. Neither Shriver nor Sam Beckworth would be displeased by a chance to kill Coleman.

A rider pounded into town from the east and swept past Coleman, riding in the middle of the street. Coleman didn't recognize him. The man went on down to the Llano and swung to the ground. He disappeared into the saloon. Although Coleman did not know it, this was Slim Edgerton, just arriving from Sloan's camp.

Coleman halted and shaped a cigarette. He looked at his hands in the dim light, curiously wondering if they were shaking. They weren't. He smiled ruefully. They should be shaking.

He stuck the cigarette between his lips, but he didn't light it. He stood quite still for a moment, thinking. You couldn't try and take a problem like this and solve it in its entirety. There were too many question marks. You had to take one thing at a time, settle that, and then move on to the next logical step.

Coleman guessed his most urgent business was Sam Beckworth. If he could find Sam, lodge him safely in jail. . . .

It would have been easier to find Sam, if Coleman could have stuck to the shadows like Sam was doing. But Coleman's pride wouldn't let him hide. And it wasn't only his pride that prevented it. It was the star on his vest. The star, the emblem of authority, belonged on the main street in plain sight, not slinking around in the darkness of an alley.

So he walked downstreet toward the Plains Hotel openly and with steady strides. He passed the Llano, which, while lighted and open, was strangely quiet.

The hotel loomed before him then, a two-story frame structure with balconies on three sides of the second floor. An outside stairway led to the balcony, and he searched for the telltale lumpiness that would mean a man was hiding there. The hotel balcony would make an excellent place for a sniper to hide. But it was too dark to see. Coleman wondered where Shriver was, where his own men were. So far, he had seen no one.

He had the uneasy feeling that someone was

watching him. He stood the feeling for a few moments while he waited there, staring at the hotel. Then, deliberately, fully aware that he would draw fire, he thumbed a match alight and touched it to the tip of his cigarette.

As the match flared, Coleman closed his eyes. By feel alone he brought the match up and drew on his cigarette. Abruptly, then, he exhaled, blowing out the match, and stepped swiftly to one side.

If he were being watched, the maneuver should draw almost instant fire. Coleman opened his eyes at once as the match went out. By closing them he had avoided the momentary blindness the flame would have caused. He kept his eyes on the hotel balcony and immediately saw a slight movement there, and the glint of faint light upon a rifle barrel.

Flame spat from the rifle's muzzle. A bullet whanged against a doorknob behind Coleman and ripped on through the door. Coleman crossed the street at a run, hoping that Sam, blinded by the flash of his rifle, would not see him. Apparently Sam didn't. Coleman reached the shadow of the hotel wall, and ducked into it silently. He heard the shuffle of steps above him on the wooden balcony as Sam changed his position.

The hotel door, facing the street, banged open. Coleman heard the peculiar cadences of Henshaw's British accent, and the answering tones of his daughter's voice. There was no hauteur in Constance tonight. She had come face to face with reality this afternoon. Men and the passions that drove them had ceased being a game to Constance. Constance's voice told Coleman that she was scared, thoroughly and completely afraid.

There were additional voices as others boiled out of the hotel. Down toward the Llano, a shout lifted. A dog, roused by the single rifle shot, began to bark out in the street.

Coleman slid along the hotel wall to the outside stairway. Stepping carefully, he started up. A step creaked under his weight. He halted immediately, listening.

Apparently Sam Beckworth had missed the sound, so intent was he on the crowd in the street before the hotel. Coleman kept going up. His head came above the level of the balcony floor and he could see Sam's lumpy, small shape ten yards away, crouched against the rail.

Not many men would have held their fire. Coleman did. Sam had fired at him with obvious intent to kill. Coleman knew he had a right to gun Sam down without warning.

But he had let Murphy's beliefs rub off on him. And he hated killing. So he inched on up the stairway until his feet rested on the flat floor of the balcony. Coleman was lightly crouched, trying to decide whether to chance a farther creeping advance, or stake all on a sudden rush.

He decided to try and halve the distance before he rushed. Sam Beckworth was a small man and a quick one. He would move instantly if he caught a sound behind him.

Coleman took a careful step, another, praying silently that no boards would creak under his feet. He had not previously drawn his gun, but he did so now.

Then, with a sound incredibly loud in the almost utter silence, a board did creak. Another man might have hesitated to see whether Sam would hear, what he would do if he did. Coleman had no hesitation in him. His muscles, already gathered, drove him forward without a pause. He saw Sam rise frantically, the rifle swinging. Coleman could see that it was going to be close. The rifle was swinging too fast.

Sam Beckworth was quick—terribly so. But the rifle barrel struck one of the balcony's pillars and then Coleman was upon him. Coleman's left hand, the one holding the gun, came down in a flashing arc. The gun barrel glanced off the side of Sam's head, nearly tearing one of his ears loose. For an instant he sagged, and in this brief, split second, Coleman wrestled the rifle from his grasp and flung it sliding across the balcony floor.

For the second time in as many days, Coleman seized Sam's arm and brought it around behind him, twisting, raising.

The pain cleared Sam's head. A gasp of agony escaped his clenched teeth. Coleman said softly: "All right, now. We'll head for the jail."

Panic made Sam's struggle suddenly violent. He cried: "For God's sake, man, Shriver's lookin' for me!"

"I know that. But you should have stuck to hunting Shriver. You shouldn't have shot at me." He stopped Sam's struggles with a cruel twist of his arm.

Sam began to babble. "Please! Please! Let me go. I'll get out of town."

"Uhn-uh. Come on." He pushed Sam ahead of him and down the stairs. He knew he was taking a risk with Sam's life as well as with his own. Neither risk bothered him any more. He expected to take risks himself and he didn't regret exposing Sam. Sam had asked for whatever he was going to get.

He shoved Sam ahead of him to the walk. Light from the hotel window fell upon them both, and the crowd before the hotel turned in sudden surprise.

Coleman heard a thunder of approaching hoofs up the street.

The thought flashed in his mind—*Shriver!*—but his brain instantly rejected that. There were too many. And Shriver would not come into town so openly.

He yelled at the frightened crowd—"Get back in the hotel!"—and saw them begin to move. His eyes probed the darkness in the direction from which the horses were coming. He was aware that they could be squatters. They could also be riders from the syndicate ranches. Either way, they constituted a threat. He started to draw away, to push Sam into the shadows and away from this light, but he knew he was too late. So he shoved Sam around and pointed his gun toward the sounds of the oncoming riders.

He heard a shout, a shout crazy with frenzy and surprise. "Coleman! By God . . . !"

A gun flared. There was a milling, furious tangle of horses and men at the edge of the dim light circle. Coleman's mind was stunned. That roaring voice could belong to but one man—Sloan. But how had Sloan found him?

It seemed an eternity that he stood there, immobile. Then he became aware of the danger to Sam Beckworth in this. He released Sam and gave him a violent fling toward the street. Sam sprawled into the dust.

Only one thing saved Coleman, that being the trouble Sloan and his riders were having with their horses, plunging, milling there in the street. The force Coleman had used to throw Sam from him he utilized to fling himself in the opposite direction, toward the hotel wall. He came against it, and rebounded, digging in his feet for a sprint into the shadows at its corner.

Another shot, and another, flared, and the bullets tore into the hotel wall inches behind him. Then, miraculously, he reached the corner and dived into darkness.

XVII

"Now!"

For Coleman, there was no sound except the roaring of Sloan's huge voice, no awareness of anything save this, his relentless nemesis. He momentarily forgot Shriver, Sam Beckworth, the others.

This was the man who had pursued him across half a continent, who had separated him from his wife, who had hounded and persecuted him for what seemed his entire life.

He was rolling in the weeds at the side of the hotel. They made crackling sounds as he rolled. Sloan's sharp ears picked up this sound and he poured his fire into the darkness blindly. Coleman got his feet under him and crouched silently for a moment, trying to decide what to do. In another moment, Sloan and his riders, believing him gone, would be combing the town for him. Shriver was somewhere about, perhaps even now behind him, drawing a bead on the silhouette Coleman's body presented against the dim light in the street.

Instinctively Coleman swung around and tried to see in the pitch blackness of the vacant lot. A rider urged his horse into the darkness and spurred past Coleman at full tilt, never seeing him, shouting hoarsely.

The contagion of the manhunt was in Sloan's men. Long months they had spent, patiently and futilely searching for him. Now they had him, and the knowledge was like a draft of strong liquor.

Coleman saw Sam Beckworth struggle to his feet in the dust of the street. Sam took a puzzled look at the still milling, mounted men, and then turned to shuffle away toward the opposite side of the street.

A gun flared orange directly opposite the Llano, plainly a rifle from its deep, sharp sound. Sam spun half around and stood facing Coleman, hunched a little, his arms hugging his belly. Somewhere a woman began to scream. The sound was eerie, a rising wail that beat against Coleman's eardrums in waves.

Again the rifle echoed in the street. This bullet made a noticeable impact against Sam Beckworth and slammed him down, limp and motionless, in the dust. The woman's screaming went on intermittently, as though she only paused for breath and then began to scream again. The bullet that had taken Sam's life apparently went on through him and struck one of the horses racked before the hotel, for the animal reared, broke his reins, and galloped out of sight toward the Canadian River bridge.

Sloan's men, at the bull-voiced, shouted command, broke away from the front of the hotel. Two of them went toward the river, leaving Sloan and the other alone. Coleman thought—*Now!*—and his gun came up, centering on Sloan's chest.

All it would take now would be one slight pull and Sloan could never bother him again. But he couldn't do it. He couldn't shoot even Sloan from this well of darkness, this black ambush. He felt a vast disgust with himself, a pure and undiluted self-revulsion. Then the chance was gone, for Sloan and his single rider swung upstreet.

The crowd surged out away from the hotel and gathered in a circle about Sam Beckworth's body. That had been Shriver's doing. Now Coleman had to get Shriver, and soon, for, if he didn't, tomorrow the war would begin in earnest with ranches burned, travelers waylaid, riders murdered.

He wondered where the fourth of Sloan's riders was, the one who had passed him so closely a few minutes before. He shrugged. Knowing what a perfect silhouette he made, he stood up and, when Sloan had gone out of sight into darkness, stepped out into the street.

He felt as though he were bathed in the glare of midday. Actually he was hardly visible in this dim light. He headed at a quick trot for the spot where Shriver had stood when he had killed Sam.

A new reluctance to kill had bothered him intensely lately. But he promised himself he wouldn't let it affect him when he faced Shriver. He would not have killed Shriver for burning out Sam Beckworth. But Shriver had killed Murphy and the star on Coleman's vest bound him to vengeance for that.

He gained the far side of the street and plunged into the shadows there, drawing a quick breath of relief. A voice called nearby—"Deputy!"—and Coleman swung nervously, gun extended, hammer thumbed back. The voice called frantically: "Hey, don't do that! I'm with you!"

He recognized the black-haired youngster's voice now, the voice of one of his own posse men. He came up beside the youth, panting a little, saying: "Where're the others?"

"Right here." The boy stood in a narrow passageway between two buildings. Behind him and beside him were the others, the posse Coleman had brought from Triple X.

He had the means here at hand to stop the fighting in the streets. He had the means to save his own life tonight. He stood utterly silent for a full two minutes, fighting with himself, fighting against the wrong decision that would be so blamed easy to make. All he had to do was to take these six and proceed to quiet the town. It was a lawman's right—the right to deputize a posse and use them as he saw fit.

But it wasn't fair to the men involved. It wasn't fair to them to involve them in his own private feud with Sloan. He said: "I don't need you now. Drift out of town."

The black-haired youngster's voice rose shrill

with protest. "Hey, you can't do that! You're in a fix!"

"Sure. But it's *my* fix. You get out of town." His voice was cold, uncompromising. He stared at the dark-haired kid until the boy's glance dropped uneasily away.

They grumbled a little, but they went, as Coleman had known they would. Most men had little stomach for blind night fighting, and he couldn't really blame them. It is hard to fight something you cannot even see.

He waited there in the mouth of the dark passageway until the sounds of their going had faded from his ears. He was alone now, truly alone. Sloan had four men, Shriver two. That made a total of eight that were out to get him.

He smiled, but he didn't really feel like smiling. This had become a grim business, and one from which he had little hope of emerging. He heard the distant rattle of the stage as it turned into this street and came thundering down it, the horses held at a full gallop. This was the stage from Mobeetie.

Coleman knew that the passage of the stage would momentarily draw all eyes, all attention. He took advantage of this to leave his niche between the buildings and slip uptown along the walk. But something he saw in the coach window stopped him as quickly as any bullet could have done. He saw a woman's white face, peering out.

Halted by what he saw, he shook his head as

though to clear it. This was impossible. That woman in the coach could not be Ruby. It was a chance resemblance, that was all. He wanted her so terribly that his mind was playing tricks on him. That was it. That must be it.

The woman's white face remained in his mind, like a picture superimposed upon another. Coleman frowned. He had no time right now for thoughts of Ruby. This business tonight required every bit of his concentration. But he couldn't get her out of his mind. He kept remembering her, kept seeing her at the wedding, and afterward as he'd ridden away.

He heard an approaching horseman, and flattened himself against the building wall.

The horseman stopped directly before him, and sat his animal staring fixedly across at the hotel. Coleman thought the man had missed him until the voice came low and cautions. "Coleman?"

Coleman was briefly silent, wary of a trap. Finally he murmured: "Yes?"

"Shriver's waiting for you over at the livery barn. He'll be alone."

Coleman chuckled mirthlessly. "Why? Why doesn't he come after me here?"

"He wants you for himself. He's afraid this other guy will get you first."

Coleman sighed. "All right. Tell him ten minutes."

"Sure. I'll tell him." The horseman waited a

moment more, then casually reined around and rode back upstreet.

Coleman was puzzled. Shriver was making it easier for him. Shriver was playing into his hands by separating himself from the hunt going on. Why?

He could discover only one reason. Shriver wanted the personal pleasure of killing him. He didn't want to chance Sloan's getting him first. Also, Shriver had a code that Sloan wouldn't understand at all. The gunfighter's code. Shriver perhaps saw in Coleman a man like himself, a man beset from all sides, with his gun his only companion. Maybe Shriver was even pondering the gunman's eternal question: *Is he faster than I am?* And he had to find out.

Coleman had to admit the possibility that Shriver had laid another trap. He wasn't above it. But Coleman also knew he'd go find out. There was no other way.

He started after the lone rider, but changed his mind and returned to the narrow passageway between the two buildings. At a run, he went along it, coming out in the trash-littered alley a moment later.

Instead of turning uptown toward the livery barn, he swung toward the river and the stage depot. He stumbled over a bushel basket filled with tin cans and went flat on his face. Fast-triggered bullets sliced through the air above him, and a man's voice lifted: "Hey! Here he is!"

A man came running down the alley, sure he had downed Coleman. Coleman rolled onto his right side, and fired at the sound of the approaching man. He heard his bullet strike, heard the man's soft grunt, and the scuffling sounds he made as he fell.

Then Coleman was up, running. A dull hopelessness was growing in him. That bit of action had been instinctive, its urgency allowing him no time for thought or hesitation. Damn them! They labeled a man "killer", and then they saw to it that he conformed to the label. They forced it on him whether he liked it or not. Now another man was dead because young Will Sloan had allowed his pride to force a quarrel.

How many more must die before the cycle stopped? Coleman ran silently, swiftly. Far behind he heard other shots. He cut through a weed-grown vacant lot and came into the street again directly across from the stage depot.

Hostlers were leading the tired teams away, and others were backing fresh teams into the traces. Walking, Coleman went across the street and stepped into the stage station.

Ruby, watching the door, saw him immediately. Her face had been white before. Suddenly, now, it lost all of its remaining color. Her eyes were wide, glad, and yearning, terrified at the same time. Coleman realized that he still held his gun. He shoved it angrily back into its holster. He crossed the room, almost running, and she met him, throwing herself eagerly and frantically into his arms. Her lips were sweet, warm, and the tears ran freely across her cheeks. Coleman said hoarsely: "I thought it was you, but I had to know."

The star on his vest bit into her smooth cheek, and she drew away, staring at it without comprehension. She read the words on it, and slow gladness came into her face that was wonderful to see. But the gladness faded before her thoughts. She said: "I've led him to you, Floyd. I didn't mean to, but I've led him to you."

"Sloan?" He gestured with his head at the door. "He'd have found me, anyway."

Ruby broke from his arms. She ran across the stage depot and began to rummage in her bag. She came up with an envelope and handed it to Coleman, whose face was puzzled. He ripped open the envelope. A glance told him what this was. A warrant. A warrant charging Sloan with the murder of Frank O'Connell, Ruby's father.

And he hadn't even known Frank was dead. He looked at Ruby with quick pity. He said: "I'm sorry, Ruby. I've brought you nothing but trouble."

Her arms went around his neck, clutching, desperate. He became aware that time was passing, that Shriver was waiting. He was also aware that Sloan might at any time take a notion to search for him here at the stage depot. He knew the agony of divided compulsion. He had no choice but to go out and finish what had been started tonight. Yet how could he leave Ruby? How could he forsake her now?

He said: "Go on up to the hotel. I'll see you there in half an hour." He tried not to let her see the doubt, the uncertainty that hung like a black cloud over his thoughts. Maybe she saw, and maybe she did not. She had heard shots in this town, she had seen his gun in his hand. She had seen the star, and she knew he had an unfinished job out there.

She gave him a wan smile and murmured without hope: "All right, Floyd. Half an hour."

XVIII

"I've Been Waiting for You"

He reached the livery barn in about four minutes, moving at a brisk walk up the alley behind the stage depot. He watched it silently for a long moment, out of the shadows across the street from it. A single lamp burned inside the stable, showing through the windows and through the cracks in the walls.

Then he stepped out into the street and began to cross. A sound to his right halted him, and he whirled nervously. A voice said: "Go on in. I'll watch out here and see you ain't interrupted." It was the voice of the horseman who had carried Shriver's message to him. Coleman walked toward him warily. "All right. But I'll take your gun. You don't need it to yell a warning."

The man hesitated, then moved quickly to one side. With abrupt and unthinking anger in him, Coleman sprang forward, drawing his gun as he did. He brought its barrel down solidly on the man's head, and then stepped away, watching without feeling as the man slumped into the street.

There was yet another, and then Shriver. Coleman wondered where the second of Shriver's followers was. He crossed the street swiftly and stepped close to the building's wall.

He heard nothing inside, so he swung open the door and stepped in. Instantly he saw Shriver down at the far end of the stable, merely a black shadow in the dimness. Shriver, he saw at once, had allowed himself a certain advantage. Coleman stood almost directly under the lamp, but Shriver was partly hidden in darkness.

Shriver's other man was the thing that bothered Coleman, not Shriver himself, although he was dangerous enough. Shriver's voice sounded strangely hollow in the huge interior of the barn. "I've been waiting for you."

Coleman asked, tense and nervous: "Where's your other man?"

Shriver laughed contemptuously.

"Gone." He hesitated a moment, then he said: "He went back to Triple X."

Coleman knew he was lying. But he didn't know whether Shriver was lying about the man's being gone, or about his going back to Triple X. Perhaps the man had rebelled against Shriver's brutality and Shriver had killed him. Or perhaps the man was here, now, hiding in the shadows to distract Coleman at the crucial moment.

He shrugged inwardly. There was little he could do to change this situation. He had to take his cards as they were dealt. He began to walk toward Shriver, carefully settling his weight on each foot before he would lift the other to step forward again. This way, he was never off balance.

His right hand hung loosely at this side, and his left was crooked slightly, tense and ready.

Shriver, too, was walking, in the same cautious way. Coleman began to talk, for he knew he still had to convince himself that this killing was unavoidable. He said: "You shouldn't have killed Murphy, Shriver. That's what I'm after you for. If it wasn't for Murphy, I might be tempted to let you go."

Shriver laughed, but there was less assurance in this laugh than there had been in the last. He grunted, still walking carefully: "You're not that good, Coleman. You'll do your best, but you'll be lucky if you get a shot off before I kill you."

Shriver speeded his pace a little. His nerves were giving way before Coleman's steady certainty. Coleman could almost smile at that. He didn't feel certain. Inside, he was churning, wanting to quit town and take Ruby with him, for only that way would he be sure of her. He was glad a man's thoughts did not show in his face.

Shriver seemed to crouch and there was a certain tightening of his facial muscles. These were the signs, the giveaway of the man's intent. Before his hand moved at all, Coleman knew that this was the time. His training took over, and his mind stopped functioning altogether. It was instinct now, and reflex. He felt the cold butt of his gun against his palm, and then the gun was out, raising.

In this, the first test of his speed since the

smashing of his right hand, he knew suddenly that a man cannot change hands and retain his full measure of skill. He was slow, maybe too slow.

But he had enough speed to make Shriver hurry. A fraction of a second too soon Shriver's gun blasted. The bullet tore through Coleman's left holster, creating a sensation of a grasping hand, clutching and slipping away. Coleman took his time. His gun centered on Shriver and bucked against his palm.

Noise behind Coleman made him whirl before Shriver had even started to fall. The big double doors of the stable burst outward. There, under the single lamp, was Sloan, and behind him his four men.

Shriver behind him, Sloan before him. Shriver was probably dead. But he might be alive, might still be able to shoot. Coleman didn't dare look. It was a chance he had to take. He snapped a shot at Sloan, but knew at once it was wide.

And then a gun blasted behind him. Shriver. Coleman stood frozen, rooted, unable to move for a long moment. He should be feeling pain. He should be falling. There should be a blackness descending over him. But he felt nothing. Was it possible that Shriver could have missed?

But then Coleman saw Sloan. The man had a stupidly furious, outraged expression on his face. He mouthed a few indistinguishable words and collapsed limply onto the manure-littered floor.

Coleman came to life. He dived to one side, found shelter in one of the horse stalls. He brought his gun up, intending to shoot. He didn't. Sloan's men stood in a group, stunned.

There was no understanding this. Coleman knew that Shriver had not missed him and hit Sloan by mistake. Shriver had killed Sloan intentionally. But why?

Coleman's brain began to click again. He yelled: "He's dead, you can see that! I'm the law here in Troncosa! I've got a warrant for Sloan here in my pocket. I'll give you fifteen minutes to get out of town. If you aren't gone by then, I'll jail you for complicity in Frank O'Connell's murder."

They stared at each other stupidly. Then, still wordless, they turned and shuffled into the outside darkness.

Coleman ran over and knelt beside Shriver. Shriver had saved his life, and he had to know why. The gunman was sprawled on his face, gun extended before him. Coleman spoke without touching him. "Why'd you do that?"

Shriver turned on his side, grimacing with pain. There was a wet, red stain that covered half his shirt front and a pool of blood where he had lain. His thin lips twisted into what might have been a grin. He looked at Coleman, and there was neither friendliness nor hatred in his glance. Just emptiness. He said: "I had a guy hounding me once like

265

that one was hounding you. I guess I shot him because I hated his breed."

Coleman knew he wanted no thanks, so he offered none. He squatted beside Shriver and waited, companionably, for the man to die. There was no use rushing off for help. Shriver was beyond help. Shriver wouldn't have asked him to stay, but no man likes to die alone. So Coleman waited, and after a while Shriver's eyes glazed and his head fell limply against the ground.

Coleman got up, and, as though sleepwalking, stalked toward the open doors. What had happened tonight was admittedly incredible. Yet here he was, and his enemies were gone, dead. He stepped over Sloan's body in the doorway, scarcely seeing it. He was not thinking of hatred, of killing, or vengeance. He was thinking of something else, of a woman's soft arms, of her misty, tear-filled eyes. He was thinking of Ruby's warm body, her eager lips. He was thinking that she was his wife, his own, and that it had been a long time, a long, long time.

He began to walk swiftly. Townspeople passed him, running toward the stable, where there had been so many shots. He didn't see them. He came around the corner and could see the Llano saloon and beyond it the Plains Hotel. He could see a woman, slim, running toward him, holding her skirts high so they would not trip her. Ruby. Without being conscious of it, Coleman began to run himself. With long, racing strides he closed the distance between them, caught her fiercely as she fled into his arms.

The hunger in Coleman was overpowering. He clutched her to him savagely. Never, never would she get farther from him than this. Never again. He lowered his mouth and tasted the full, sweet promise of her lips. He knew a rich satisfaction and a joy in living. Running was finished. Now, his guns were only tools, the tools with which a lawman preserved the peace. Murphy had been right and Coleman knew he would be forever and eternally grateful.

About the Author

Lewis B. Patten wrote more than ninety Western novels in thirty years, and three of them won Spur Awards from the Western Writers of America, and the author received the Golden Saddleman Award. Indeed, this points up the most remarkable aspect of his work: not that there is so much of it, but that so much of it is so fine. Patten was born in Denver, Colorado, and served in the U.S. Navy, 1933-1937. He was educated at the University of Denver during the war years and became an auditor for the Colorado Department of Revenue during the 1940s. It was in this period that he began contributing significantly to Western pulp magazines, fiction that was from the beginning fresh and unique and revealed Patten's lifelong concern with the sociological and psychological affects of group psychology on the frontier. He became a professional writer at the time of his first novel, *Massacre at White River* (1952). The dominant theme in much of his fiction is the notion of justice, and its opposite, injustice. In his first novel it has to do with exploitation of the Ute Indians, but as he matured as a writer he explored this theme with significant and poignant detail in small towns throughout the early West. Crimes, such as rape or lynching, are often at the center of his stories. When the values embodied in these small towns are examined closely, they are found to be wanting. Conformity is always easier than taking a stand. Yet, in Patten's view of the American West, there is usually a man or a woman who refuses to conform. Among his finest titles, always a difficult choice, are surely *Death of a Gunfighter* (1968), *A Death in Indian Wells* (1970), and *The Law at Cottonwood* (1978). No less noteworthy are his previous Five Star Westerns, *Tincup in the Storm Country*, *Trail to Vicksburg*, *Death Rides the Denver Stage*, *The Woman at Ox-Bow*, and *Ride the Red Trail*.

Additional Copyright Information

Center Point Publishing
600 Brooks Road • PO Box 1
Thorndike ME 04986-0001 USA

(207) 568-3717

**US & Canada:
1 800 929-9108**
www.centerpointlargeprint.com